PRAISE FOR THE CRITICAL LIST

What's so attractive about John Wenke's stories is their stare-you-down directness—Wenke's unflinching, deft (and welcome) conviction about the transportive and redeeming power of what we used to call *good old American realism*.

– Richard Ford

These stories showcase smart, resourceful people at the end of their rope, radically reshaping their lives. Within the familiar worlds of home and neighborhood, John Wenke uncovers violence, yearning, and comedy. Yes, there's always something funny, even when the situation's critical. A brilliant collection, where "…everything is calm until everything explodes."

– Cary Holladay, author of *Brides in the Sky: Stories and a Novella*

The stories in John Wenke's *The Critical List* take a look at Americans taking a look at their own mortality. The title comes from the things some of his characters talk about—"a freefall of small and large miseries"—as they try (without success) to stop the advance of time. In one of Wenke's stories, a boy keeps his father alive by befriending his ghost; in yet another, a drunken attempt at a criminal scheme ends up in a hilarious Christmas celebration. "Trouble keeps happening" to Wenke's characters, but they keep fighting back, resilient and undaunted. These stories make up an American atlas, a road map from Connecticut to California. Get your copy now. John Wenke's tough-minded, big-hearted America awaits your discovery.

– John Surowiecki, author of *Pie Man*, winner of the 2017 Nilson Prize for a First Novel

THE CRITICAL LIST

John Wenke

Regal House Publishing

Published by
Regal House Publishing, LLC
Raleigh, NC 27612
All rights reserved

ISBN -13 (paperback): 9781947548985
ISBN -13 (epub): 9781646030255
Library of Congress Control Number: 2019941547

Interior and cover design by Lafayette & Greene
lafayetteandgreene.com
Cover images © by Mr Doomits / Shutterstock

Regal House Publishing, LLC
https://regalhousepublishing.com

Printed in the United States of America

To Sheila and our children—
Jacqueline, Joseph, Benjamin and Gabriel

Contents

Choke Hold

Marsha Flinders gnaws the slivered nail jutting from the jagged crescent of her left index finger. Though biting hard, she merely snips some skin. Blood seeps into the flayed cuticle.

"Ouch!" Shoving her finger into her mouth, she stretches her neck to see around a gaggle of squawking hens—her crowd—stationed in the cluttered aisle between the small food court and Space Mania's big attraction—a play-maze caged in netting that resembles the wire mesh restraining the leaping, hooting spider monkeys in the downtown zoo. Marsha's eyes scour their capering cousins, these primates predisposed toward credit card bankruptcies, hate crimes, competitive eating, and bingo. They caterwaul through twisted tubes, somersault down padded inclines, and thrash in pits of multi-colored plastic balls. Like a pivoting surveillance camera, Marsha's head rotates, but she can't find Kenny. Her throat muscles tighten; he's either crawling through a tube, disappearing into space dust, or being raped by a pedophilic slayer.

"Hey, Sally!" Marsha's voice makes no dent in Space Mania's pay-for-play din of squealing kids, screaming parents and ringing arcade bells. With her throbbing leg propped, she sits at the edge of the five-table eatery. Behind her, burgers spit on the griddle. A blender churns ice cream. A girl bickers with her friend.

"I got here first."

"No, you didn't!"

"I *did.*"

Marsha takes her finger out of her mouth and bellows, "Sally! Sally Cooble!"

One of the hens turns, smiles and bends an ear. "What is it, Marsh?"

In this gang—the mothers assembled for Sarah Hart's sixth birthday party—all you get is one syllable: Sally is Sal; Cynthia is Cyn; Bernadette is Bern; Marsha is Marsh.

"I can't see Kenny. Is he still there? Can you see him?"

"You just relax. We've all been keeping an eye on him. He's right over there. On the flight deck. Waiting in line."

"Really? Thanks."

Marsha fakes a smile, plants a crutch on the sticky orange tile floor, and hoists herself on her right leg. With her left leg still propped, she peers around three laughing men. Two overweight boys are jostling Kenny out of the way. Jungle Law. In the bush, the bullies would be hyenas and Kenny a lame gazelle. Her raven eyes rend flesh, but Marsha resists the urge to swoop in like a henish harpy—a bedraggled avenger with slashing crutches in lieu of cutting claws. Now safely behind the bullies, Kenny bumps in and out of view. Marsha squints. He's bobbing his head, but she can't tell if he's moving his lips.

In the mobbed command center, the kids are strafed by flashing lights. They shove one another to get a crack at the reclining seats fronting the control panel. Here a Space Ranger might steer the ship, fire laser bolts at alien spacecraft, or radio crisis reports to Earth Central. Or a tired ranger might just lie in one of five glass-encased deep-sleep space couches. The bullies scatter into two open seats, leaving Kenny next in line. He turns and gestures behind a little red-haired boy, who is pointing a remote-control device at a robot covered with blinking lights. The robot flaps his arms, takes two steps forward, two steps back, and then bows from the waist. To the left of the control window, a little girl, her hair flared with wild ringlets, snuggles to the keyboard, punches prefabricated questions into the Super Cryptillion Computer and receives prefabricated answers. His turn comes; Kenny settles into one of the captain's chairs. He pushes some buttons, making asteroids and planets explode. Sitting next to him is Sarah Hart, a skinny blond with cropped hair and a pouting face. She has both hands on a Nuclear Kill Laser Bazooka.

With neck aching, Marsha plops back, exhausted, her temples pulsing. The back of her neck burns like heated coils. Her throat growls. Squirming in the wobbly pink molded seat, her ears tortured by the sonic percussion—that howitzer whiffing—blasting from the Death-to-Aliens videogame, she wiggles her behind and steadies the fiberglass cast squeezing her swollen left ankle. It rests on a blue chair with uneven legs. Her right arm straddles a rickety table. No sooner does she settle into place than the blue chair clacks and sends her heel skating. A razor-sharp pain slices her leg. A few seconds pass before the rippling pain settles into the usual throb. With feathery fingers, she rattles the plastic tube in her shirt pocket. Not forty minutes ago, two hours too soon, she doubled her dose and now she wants more.

Behind her the Death-to-Aliens box whoops. Frenzied wonking booms like sixteen spastic tubas. A human voice barges in.

"YAHYAHYAHYAHYAH!"

Marsha jolts upright. Her ankle skitters, jazzed with a thousand volts. Her breath sucks in. She needs to kill that kid, or maybe just chop off his hands and tongue.

"YAHYAHYAHYAH!"

As Marsha cranks her head around, little needles prick the nerves running from ankle to brain. A string bean boy of about thirteen jumps up and down—"YAHYAHYAHYAH!" On his forehead, a boil flares. Pimples dot his throat.

Marsha reins in her rage and tries the civil approach. She sounds like her mother.

"Young man! Excuse me, please. I'd like a word with you."

The boy still jumps and screams. From the red seat beside her, Marsha picks up a napkin dripping with mustard, crumples it, and pops the boy in the head. "Yo, punk!"

A dab of mustard clashes with splayed purple dye.

Boil Boy turns and stops screaming. He scrunches his nose like a spider monkey lost in spider monkey thought, puzzled by the startling sight of a woman near thirty scowling—and now shouting—at him from the other side of the mesh.

"Keep the racket down, punk! You're giving me a headache. You know what a headache is? I'll come over and give you one."

Marsha shakes her crutch.

The twitching vein in Boil Boy's neck reminds Marsha of what happens to Bill when he's about to lose it—the same vein, the same jiggle. But Boil Boy doesn't let go. His mouth sags into an oval, all shocked to hell that some bitch is calling him down, his mind on seven-second delay, all gummed up, a churning jumble of junk, like *what the fuck? Did that bitch just give me some shit?*

"You talkin' to *me?*"

Marsha laughs. The punk filched a movie line. Where's it from? Some tough guy talking tough to make himself sound tougher. *Taxi Driver.* Mohawk gunner man mowing down the scum.

"I sure am, punk. Look at me!" She's channeling Chili Palmer, even puffs her cheeks, blowfish style, to affect Travolta's chubbed-out face. "I'm tellin' you to keep your voice down. And if I have to tell you again, I'll wipe the floor with you."

"Fuck *you!*" Boil Boy points a finger at her face and pulls the trigger. "Know what I mean? I mean, fuuuuuck *you!*"

Marsha can't believe it when this big hand grabs Boil Boy by the throat, lifts him straight off the floor, and throws him an easy four feet. Throws him right through the air. It's like something you'd see in a cartoon. Boil Boy hits the wall. The popcorn maker wobbles. White puffy mounds tumble into little heaps. But Boil Boy doesn't bounce. He slides to his haunches and screams.

"Hey, Da-ad! What ya doin'? Tryin' to kill me?"

"Shut up!"

The punk's old man is laughing, stroking his chin, waving his left hand, inviting the kid to fight. The guy stands all of six-five with slicked-back graying hair, a former pumper turning to suet. His round face is red and beery with flabby Fred Flintstone cheeks and take-me-to-your-leader brows. A new moon scar runs from his left ear to the edge of his mouth. He gives Marsha a mouth-breathing smile and turns to the boy, now sliding up the wall, cowering, his head bent sideways and eyes bulging.

"Have a little couth when somebody asks you to shut up! Don't you see this pretty lady's got a problem? Now get the hell away before I slap you one."

"But Da-ad! I won two games. Two games!"

The old man boxes the air and steps toward his son. "Get your ass out of here!"

Boil Boy squirms to full height and bolts.

Seconds later, the guy sits on the red chair. When his knee grazes hers, she moves it. His knee follows and knocks it. He's the hunter. She's his meat.

Yesterday, Marsha left her wedding ring on the deck in a stinking tuna fish can she set atop Bill's clothes and his pathetic pile of movables—an Indian River High School yearbook, seven Elmore Leonard paperbacks, a five-string electric guitar and a box of heavy metal CDs. With Marsha directing, an ebullient Kenny had dumped Bill's things out of the upstairs window. As of this morning, he hadn't come back to get more of the message. Thursday night, after she had told Kenny to call 911, Bill banged out of the house. While she talked to the dispatcher, he revved his heap car—all boom, grumbles, and explosive farts—and roared away. Marsha didn't want Bill to die, exactly, just disappear, end the story, not leave it like it is now—everything suspended, her throat tight, almost strangled, with no wedding ring and a large hunter to fend off, worried that Bill might have read the kitchen calendar and come slinking into the play place, all hangdog and sorry and wondering what she said to the cops. Then she'd have the problem of getting rid of him all over again.

But there weren't any cops that night, only the paramedics. In less than seven minutes they had made the run east on Route 50 from Peninsula Regional Medical Center.

At the bottom of the steps, naked beneath her clutch of blankets, Marsha watched Meg, a butch-looking woman who turned out to be a grandmother, use gentle hands and slide a board beneath her crooked ankle.

"How'd ya fall?"

"My husband and I had an argument. When I was stomping down the steps to sleep on the couch, I tripped over something." She looked at Kenny. He was in his Power Rangers pajamas, crying, holding Rufus, his Teddy Bear.

"She fell over Rufus. I left him on the stairs. It was an accident." Kenny looked squarely at Meg. "It wasn't Daddy's fault. He tried to catch her, but she fell through his arms."

Meg rolled her eyes at Fulton, a young black guy with a shaved head and thin mustache. He was crouching near the stretcher, ready to slide a big polished board under her body as soon as the ankle was stabilized.

"Your husband?" he said, clearing his throat, his nose snuffling like he smelled something bad. "Did he, like, give you a little push and *then* try to catch you?"

Marsha's ankle tilted. Her body spasmed.

"No, Bill stayed upstairs. I came down. *I* tripped. He's basically a coward and doesn't have the guts to push me." She smiled and shivered. "He hates me and Kenny."

"Marsha," Meg said. "We have shelters, if you think you're suffering abuse. Good places, too. Safe. I can put you through to my friend Nell. She's with the Life Crisis Center up in Seaford. It'll be discrete."

"No, it's nothing like that. It's other stuff."

"Well," Fulton huffed," if he didn't *do* this, then where *is* the man? He picked a bad time to take a fade."

6

"I told him to leave forever, and he left."

Bill had thought it was funny—Marsha naked at the bottom of the steps with a busted ankle. He'd said, "Well, I guess there's a God after all."

She'd screamed, "If you don't go away, I'll tell Daddy to kill you. I'll tell him what you've been doing to me and he'll either kill you himself or have one of his friends kill you. He knows how to do it, so he won't get caught."

Bill had blanched, his weasel eyes flashing panic. He was afraid of her father. Before going to Vietnam, her father had ridden with the Pack Rats, a cycle gang from Newark, Delaware. In the war he was a grunt, all snout and claws, weed and skag. After two tours, he came home strung out. He hit bottom and did a month in jail for aggravated assault, but then he got straight and split with the Pack. After Marsha was born, he married her mother and worked as an auto mechanic for his father-in-law. Bart Mason now owned Walker Exxon on Route 13 in Harrington, Delaware, and made big bucks towing cars for AAA, but he'll occasionally dusted off his chopper and ran down to Dewey Beach with a few old guys from the Pack, the lifers.

Meg had her ankle and leg taped to the board.

"Fulton, time to lend a hand. Gentle does it."

Fulton slipped both hands under her thighs and Meg lifted under her arms, blanket and all. They slid her on to the big board. Within seconds, the paramedics set it on the stretcher.

"Why am I so cold? I'm all shaky."

"Shock, dear," Meg said. "It's normal."

Fulton cleared his throat.

"Is there anybody we can call? To meet us at the ER, I mean. they might need to put you under to set the bones. Is there somebody who can take care of the boy? He can ride with us all right, but he shouldn't just hang there. We can leave a note here for his daddy. He might come back."

"He's not my daddy," Kenny squeaked. "He's only my

stepfather. Daddy's over there." Kenny pointed to the foyer. "He says he wants to help push Mommy to the ambulance."

Marsha was sweating and shivering, She was about to scream.

"Six months ago, my Sam was eating lunch while driving between open houses. He always ate too fast. Somehow, a cheeseburger got caught in his throat and he choked to death. The car crashed into a pole over near St. Francis de Sales church. Last month, I went crazy and married Bill. I dated him back at Indian River. Since then, Kenny talks to his father." Marsha shrugged and shivered. "Maybe he does."

Fulton studied the ceiling and cracked his knuckles. Meg licked her lips and nodded. She reached over, grabbed Kenny by the arm and squashed him to her side.

"You're a lucky little boy. My daddy's been gone five years, and I'd give anything to talk to him."

Fulton cleared his throat. "Hey, we need to split. That ankle needs work. If you don't want Bill involved, can we leave the boy at a neighbor's?"

"No! I'm going," Kenny screamed. "I'm going. I'm going." He leaped and clamped his arms around Marsha's neck. He stared at the foyer and screamed. "Tell them to let me go!" He paused. "Daddy says you have to let me go."

Marsha pushed him away.

"All right already, just get the phone. I'll call grandma and grandpop." She looked at the paramedics. "They're forty miles from here, but they'll come right away. He'll be good."

Boil Boy's dad knocks her knee and pats it over and over.

With a disgusted grunt, Marsha lifts her right leg and tries to swing it over her cast, but on the slippery seat she tilts in the guy's direction. To stop herself, she plants her right foot, scrunches up, and jerks the entire chair six inches to the left. A canyon of air opens. He scoots his knee across the great divide and pats her knee again and again.

"Just relax," he says. "I can see you're stressed. That kid of mine'll do it to anybody. He acts like he was raised in a hog pen. No effing manners. By the way, my name is Jim, but my friends call me Duff, short for Duffy."

He stops patting her knee and wants to shake. Marsha ignores his paw, inhales deeply, and blows out slowly. Of late, the pressing presence of men in heat has been making her sick. She wonders if she's turning into one of those New Virgin icicles her mother told her she saw on *Oprah*. Sex aversion. And why not? Every time she shuts her eyes, Bill's hairy ass looms like a mutant face on a painted fun house balloon.

"I'm Polly," Marsha says. "Short for Polly. Excuse me."

She grabs her crutches and raises herself on one foot.

"Can I help you?"

"Nobody can help me. I need to see my son."

She settles her chaffed armpits into the rubber rests. Her ankle hangs like a bulging mass of constricted foam. Kenny isn't in the control room. Her eyes rotate to the rope ladder. There. Climbing hand over hand, Kenny nods his head and laughs. He points over his shoulder with his thumb. Reaching the top, he pauses at the entrance to the maze of tubes. Stepping aside and waving his hand, he lets his father go first.

"Are you all right?" Duff grips her elbow. He's in her face.

Marsha spins and squints. Beneath the livid white scar, his missed whiskers sprout like clumps of black and gray spikes.

"I'm fine and dandy. I was just looking for my son, but I can't find him. He must be going down one of the slides."

Her head wobbling, she settles into her seat. "In about a minute I'm going to have to find him."

"I don't *want* to know what my kid's doing, the son of a bitch." Duff laughs. "If there's any trouble, they find me."

But now the thought of running from this lug irks her. Who's he to make *her* scuttle? She'd hunt the hunter.

Her voice hikes to her business tone. "That boy did strike me as a problem child. I don't think I could stand it. There's talk now—I heard it on *All Things Considered*—of retroactive birth control. Besides, there are too many males in the world. Just go to any bar and you'll see the surplus stock fattening up at the trough."

Duff laughs, throwing back his head.

"You sound like a libber." He slaps his knee. "But you got one thing right. He *is* a problem child, but I don't have to see him much. Just every other weekend. I'd go back to court to change it to every *third* weekend, but my ex-old lady'd shoot me."

In an open field, a fat lady in an oversized red and black flannel shirt steadies her rifle and takes careful aim. It's a perfect day for a turkey shoot.

"Throwing him against the wall worked, but what do you do when you don't have a wall?"

Marsha watches Boil Boy turn into a large balloon tied to a Thanksgiving Day float. A clown with a machete slices the strings. With a little wobble, the boy drifts toward space.

"Usually, I just let him do whatever he effing wants. I mean, hey, it's only a few hours and he *is* my kid, you know. He likes to come to this place, so I bring him. At least he ain't off smoking crack." His laugh lines twitter. "Or maybe he is."

Marsha's inside the body of a gorilla, squatting on Duff, hindquarters to chest. Her long hairy fingers wrap around his throat, squeezing the laughing face until it bulges like a waterlogged tomato. Then it explodes. Splat, splatter.

"It's been very nice talking to you, but I—"

"You want to know something? You don't look like a mother."

"Well, I am."

"I mean, you don't look like the other mothers, all burnedout and plain. Haven't I seen you somewhere before?"

"Pa-leese!" Then the gorilla snarls. "There really *are* too many men in the world. It's why there are all these wars."

Duff is scratching his head. Dandruff flutters like mist.

"I'm sure I seen you. You dance, right? At that Seaford place. The Come On Inn. You go by the name Autumn. I recognize the short black hair. How you move it. I always wanted to talk to you."

"I've never been there and I don't dance. Besides, why would I want to wiggle my butt and all in front of a lot of drunks? Didn't your mother ever tell you? If you let losers look at you naked, you absorb them. It's like you're some kind of sponge."

The shutter clicks and she's atop the bar in front of Duff, decked out in her father's old army fatigues, boots and all, kicking away drinks and stomping his fingers into flattened worms. She smiles. His brows twitch. Behind that wall, he must be sizing her up as a crazy bitch, pretty but nuts with a mouth the size of an effing tunnel.

"Hey, you know, it ain't like that. Not everybody's drunk. When you get down to it, it's only about entertainment."

"Well, it's only about sex." She smiles. "You should talk to my second husband. He's your kind of fella."

Every night, Bill had to pump her, like it was the law or something. But he didn't do that right away. The Bermuda honeymoon was okay. But after they got back, Kenny started talking to Sam and Bill got mean. He didn't like it when Marsha asked Kenny about Sam as if Sam was in the room. It was a sick game that brought Sam back, but she stopped playing when she saw it wasn't a game to Kenny. She can see why it got to Bill. After four dates, he had quick-married a widow, who wouldn't change her name and preferred the company of her dead husband's ghost. His response was to turn himself into a machine, all spindle, shaft and piston. Bill liked to twist her into a Gumby doll—legs up there, arms out there, bend over, sit up. On the day Marsha broke her ankle, Bill started calling Kenny "Spook." *Hey, Spook, what's the ghost wearing?* He'd also started singing the Ghostbusters jingle. *Who do ya call? Ghostbusters!*

What ended it, what got her out of bed and running down the stairs, was when Bill taunted Sam.

He had just pumped her, and then he told her to roll over and kneel. She punched him in the chest and told him to bug off, but he flipped her over and propped her up. His thing slapped her from behind.

"Okay, Sam Flinders, watch this! Marsha, time to bark!"

"Whaddaya mean, husband?" Duff grunts. "You don't have a husband. You don't have a wedding ring."

"Wanna bet? I got an engagement ring, a wedding ring, and a five-year anniversary band. They're off being sized. I recently lost fifty pounds. I'm a champion biggest loser. I'm going on tour a week from Friday. It's a wonder what the power of positive thinking and no ice cream can do. By the way, I promised my son we'd have some ice cream. It's been a lovely time."

"You need a hand? I could get people out of your way."

"No thanks. People hear me coming. Clack. Clack. Clack."

"Hi, Mommy."

Kenny has her straight black hair but not her round face. His eyes sparkle. Talking to his father has made him a happy child, though he constantly pulls his fingers as if plucking flowers out by the roots. Maybe one of these days she'll take him to see somebody. Her mother says it's his way of adjusting. Her father thinks Kenny's psycho, that moving Bill in knocked his screws loose. When she was in the emergency room, she told her dad she was done with Bill. He said, "You're finally thinking right. All that bum ever did was grab. He's after your house and insurance money, but I'll see to it he don't get a dime."

"Hey," Duff laughs. "Now you don't have to find him."

"Mommy, I need to go to the bathroom. They're going into the party room soon."

"You having fun, darling?"

"It's great. Daddy's waiting in the tunnel."

Kenny runs off.

"Well, I'll be damned!" Duff mumbles. "I didn't think you were telling the truth. I didn't think you were still married."

"I am. More than you know."

"But I didn't think they let adults inside that thing. Me—I wouldn't effing fit."

"My husband's on the small side. You could be right next to him and not even know he's there."

"Well, hell, I guess I'll see you." Duff slaps both knees, gets up and drifts backwards. "Take care of that leg, Polly. By the way, how'd you do it?"

Marsha grins. "You wouldn't believe it. Last week we were skiing in Aspen. I was bending left to take a curve and my bindings flew off. I just lifted into space and didn't think I'd ever come down."

As soon as Duff sidles into a mob of kids and adults, Marsha Flinders claws into her pocket. The pills rattle. She squints: *This medication may impair your ability to operate machinery.* Her ankle, however, is a pulsing pod of pain. With a push and a spin she lifts the cap. Two little pills skitter into her palm. She's due one pill at five. Two more now puts her four over the limit. With a nod of her head, she resolves not to take any more till ten.

Slipping the pills on her tongue, she hoists herself up, crutches to a water fountain and laps the arching stream. She gags. Swallowing is getting harder all the time. Everything she tastes is just another burger choking Sam to death.

"Hey, Marsh!"

Sally Cooble is there, happy as hell to be of service.

"It's time to get to the party room. Let me help."

"I'm fine."

Sally shoves and kicks the plastic chairs.

"Comin' through! Out of the way, people!"

The way opens. In clear space Marsha achieves a metronomic rhythm. Children and parents wait behind a young man in a silver space suit. Sally waves them on and they turn down a corridor, heading toward pizza, song, games and cake. At Space Station Three, they file in. Twenty chairs span the perimeter. With Sally gripping her elbow, Marsha settles into one.

From the middle of the ceiling hangs a beach ball replica of planet Earth. The walls are covered with red, purple, and orange planets stenciled on a black field dotted with stars. There are yellow constellations and clustered galaxies, tumbling asteroids and fiery meteors, wayward moons and cruising comets. A spaceship, outward bound, bears the name Party Express.

"This guy Gil's a major flake," Sally whispers.

Captain Gil is scattering nine children around eight chairs.

"I hate musical chairs," Marsha fumes. "It's so predatory. I was always the first kid out. The music stopped and I'd freeze."

The *Star Wars* theme explodes, and the children march in circles. They all touch the chairs, ready to pounce.

"By the way, how's Kenny doing?" Sally's voice lilts, as if nothing's intended. Everybody knows Kenny talks to Sam, though nobody mentions it. They all think she was crazy to marry Bill, though everyone acted excited.

"Tell me the truth, Sal. Do you think he needs a shrink?"

This bluntness clogs Sally up. Nobody's ready for the truth. She sputters. "What do you mean?" Her words are fish bones snagged in her throat.

"Is he nuts because he talks to Sam? Mom thinks it's a phase, but Dad says I made Kenny crazy by marrying Bill. What do *you* think?"

Already, Kenny has been squeezed from the game. He stands next to Saturn. His mouth is moving. He laughs.

"I don't know. I figure it's something he'll grow out of. If you take him to a shrink, they'll just put him on Ritalin. It happened to my niece. If I were you, I don't think I'd do anything. I'm with your mother. How *is* she, by the way?"

"I haven't done anything because maybe Sam really *is* there, and I just can't see him. I don't have the eyes."

Her chair dips eight feet, but her mind lifts off like a zig-zagging kite.

"I'd try not to worry about it. He misses his father. A lot's changed."

The kite collides with a comet and flops to the ground. Marsha decides to feed the hens some high caloric gossip. Fat to chew. Fat to burn.

"It's still changing. The night I broke my ankle, I kicked Bill out. I'm afraid he might come back, and if he does I'll kick him out again. Even if they make me split the insurance money, he's a goner."

Two children huddle next to Kenny. Marsha's head wobbles.

"I see now he was just a predator. Right after Sam died, he called me to talk. For three months, he nagged me to go out with him, and then I figured what the hell. It turned into a loopy back-to-the-past thing. It was crazy. He wanted sex all the time. He's one of those sex addicts. It makes me sick."

Sally beams. Later the phones will fry.

"You should've talked to me about it. Sure, you went to the prom with him, but in the meantime, Bill Mellon had those three other marriages. Mert and I always figured he was after the money. By the way, you should talk to Mert. When it comes to business, he's all shark."

"Thanks, but Daddy has lawyers. He hates Bill."

"I think when marriages last less than a month, there's some kind of legal mumbo-jumbo where they can wipe the thing away."

"I need to rest my eyes." Her head has become a cinderblock. "I take these Percocet pills and suddenly just get sleepy."

In a half-snooze, she barely notices the party rushing on. Nan's daughter Jill wins musical chairs. The children sing six or seven party tunes. They get in a circle and play Hot Potato. Occasionally, Sally pats Marsha's wrist. Sarah Hart sits in a captain's chair and opens her presents—a profusion of Barbie dolls, Beanie Babies, books, pajamas. Marsha hears the party sounds as if muffled by a thick wall. She's conscious of Captain Gil herding the children to the table, where they sit and ogle the cake. They sing. He cuts the cake. As cold air wafts her neck, Marsha lifts from her swoon to see the children being turned into dogs.

"Everybody get your face right into the cake," Captain Gil giggles, "and let's see who can eat it the fastest."

Every child chows down, slavering and burrowing, muzzle white and lapping. Marsha tilts up, aggravated, and looks down the line to see most of the hens laughing and pointing, though Sally Cooble is telling Mr. Hart on her right, "This just makes my blood boil!"

Captain Gil is on his feet, clapping hands.

"Who'll be first? Who'll be first?"

Kenny chokes once and gags. His hands flail. When he tries to spit and can't, Marsha pushes to one foot. A horde of parental hands seem to flap in space. One man slams Kenny's back. With eyes bulging and still unable to breathe, Kenny grabs his throat. Marsha leaps across the table, her left ankle knocking the edge. He is shaking his head back and forth as she slides chest first across the table. Marsha grabs Kenny by the back of the neck and shoves her forefinger—flayed cuticle and all—down his throat. She rakes out a gob of packed cake. With her other hand, she smashes his back. His face bulging red, Kenny gags again and the rest of the cake spews into Marsha's face. His breath heaves and he sobs, sobs, and sobs again. Marsha gathers his face in her hands.

Mr. Hart is snapping his fingers under Captain Gil's nose.

"You almost killed this kid and wrecked my girl's party."

Captain Gil rushes over and pats Marsha on the back.

"Is he okay? We were only playing."

When she feels his fingers rub her bra strap, she spins and clamps her hands around his throat. She tries to squeeze, but he backs off and pushes her away. She loses her grip and totters from the table. Sally reaches to catch her, but she falls right through her hands. Landing full weight on her left foot, she screams, twists like a top and tumbles.

"Grandpop and Grandma are coming to get us."

She gets off the phone and flops next to Kenny. She sets her crutches against a mailbox and shakes her head to fight off the gravitational pull of slumber. They are sitting on a bench down the strip from Space Mania. The management was very sorry, though not sorry enough to give Mr. Hart his money back. He's still in there screaming. "They ought to be here in about an hour. Grandpop'll drive our car."

"Can I drive with him?"

"Sure."

"Where we going?"

"Home with them."

Behind them is Delmar Pizza. She intends to buy a large pie with everything on it. While they are waiting, maybe she'll be able to help Kenny eat it. Above the sea of dirty cars, the late afternoon air drifts hazy and white under the blue sky.

"I'm glad. I like Grandma's house." Kenny shakes his bag of party favors. "I like it better than ours."

"Maybe we'll have to get a new one."

"Is he coming back?"

Marsha hugs him and clears the swelling in her throat.

"Daddy can't come back, darling. Not so I can see him, anyway."

"I mean Bill."

"Don't worry about him. It was Mamma's big mistake, but we're through with him." Her father is getting a locksmith to change all the locks. Monday he'll get his favorite lawyer in on the hunt. Everything else will be numbers. "I need to rest for awhile and you need to go out with Grandpop and tow some cars. Earn us a living, for God's sake."

"Grandpop lets me push the button. Daddy used to let me beep the horn."

Marsha pulls in her breath and steadies her head.

"Is he here, Kenny? I mean, right now, the way you see him."

She looks hard at the mailbox and wonders if Sam's ghost is sitting on top, feet dangling, arms folded. It's the sort of thing he'd do.

"He's not here right now. He was in the party room. When I was choking, he was holding me and hitting me on the back, but he left before we did. He said he had a lot to do. He said we all had a lot to do."

CLOSETS

When the banging on the front door started, my father was in the middle of one of his TV tantrums.

"You gave the thing away!" he screamed, flinging himself backwards on the couch. His foot knocked the glass top of the coffee table. A decanter filled with marbles spun, tumbled, and shattered. The marbles spilled, clattering and rolling across the hardwood floor. "I can't believe it! Again! You gave the thing away! It's fixed. It's gotta be fixed."

In the last two minutes, the Sixers had turned the ball over three times and missed four free throws. With 4.8 seconds left, the Sixers had no time-outs and had to inbound the ball under the Lakers' basket. Garner made a perfect inbounds pass to the wrong team. Kobe crossed in front of Iverson—thank you very much—drove the lane and dunked. Slammo jammo. Lakers 101, Sixers 100. When the horn sounded, my father went bonkers. Then the front knocker clacked and now the chimes were ringing.

I was sort of frozen in motion, moving and not really getting there, watching my father, worrying that he would finally kick in the television. I headed toward the front door, slow-fast, around the furniture, on tiptoe, careful not to wheel off on the marbles, glad that Mom and my two sisters hadn't gotten back from the mall. This way, they wouldn't be upset with the noise and breakage and Mom wouldn't threaten to have Dad committed. It wasn't sane, she always said, to get so worked up over sports, not to mention his health and the medical fact that men in their forties regularly dropped dead from stress.

I was especially glad that Mom and Jan and Alice (she's my twin) were still getting Jan's dress for the Junior Prom, because I figured I'd be able to get the marbles up and the place straight and Dad simmered down and settled in for our ten p.m. fill of interesting disasters as brought to us by BBC *World News*: the earthquake in Japan with ten thousand dead; the latest wilding in New York City; the follow-up report on the airliner that blew a door at thirty thousand feet and sucked a carpet magnate into the engine. These things didn't tee Dad off. They relaxed him, made him grateful for the basics, like we were all healthy and had one another and made enough money (my father being an accident attorney and people needing to sue one another, in good times and bad).

But there'd be no BBC *World News* tonight. The evening news was about to make a house call.

The banging on the door sounded like hammers. As I slipped down three waxy steps to the foyer, I saw the door flip back and two cops come barging in, guns drawn, one yelling "Everybody hold 'em up!" I froze for real and threw up my hands, figuring this was it, I'm finished, but the cops—who can figure?—they hustled past me, like I was invisible. I unfroze, hands still high, and turned.

Dad was hunched over, picking up marbles, his head snapping back and forth between the floor and screen. He was still yelling, taking in the nightmare no-escape of slow-mo replay. "Look, Ted! All he has to do is throw the ball the length of the court. It hits somebody's hands and we win. No, he's gotta try a finesse pass under *their* basket."

The skinny cop yelled, "Down on the floor!"

My father, as excitable as he got over sports—his "outlet," as he liked to tell Mom—was usually pretty calm. The sight of the two cops startled but didn't frighten him. Vietnam had made him hard to scare. He'd been an infantry lieutenant and led a platoon of tunnel rats. Fear, he once told me, got squeezed right the hell out of him.

My father didn't drop to the floor, though he did put up his hands. "What are you guys doing here?"

"Where's the woman?" this big cop wanted to know. The skinny cop, I could see, was scared. His hand was shaking.

"If you mean my wife, she's out shopping."

My father smiled really wide, lifting his hands high, talking to the big cop, but watching the skinny guy's gun. The big cop had already lowered his gun.

"We're answering a 911," the big cop said. "A woman—a Mrs. White—called in to say Doug was trying to kill Jerry."

Last weekend Doug had told me he wanted to do that. Jerry was Mr. White, Doug's dad.

"Damn it!" Dad snapped and pointed. "You got the wrong house. They live next door. That way!"

The cops turned and ran out. My father was right behind. I didn't wait to be asked along. As I skittered across the patio, I saw my mother's car coming up the drive. She probably got all shook up seeing the cop car on the lawn, me and Dad hustling for the hedges as the cops tore toward the street and ducked under the trees. I felt strange about the front door being left wide open, and the broken decanter, and marbles everywhere.

As me and Dad squeezed through a hole in the thick hedges—the cops were taking the long way around—I wondered whether Doug really was going to kill his father. "He said he'd do it."

"Do what?" Dad asked.

"Kill him!"

"Don't let Barney and Andy hear you say that."

He meant Barney Fife and Andy Taylor of Mayberry—two joke cops from an old TV show we still got on cable. My father once said there was nothing wrong with the show except the jokes weren't funny and the actors all resembled dogs.

"He said he was going to get a gun."

As we came out of the hedge hole, I tripped over a root and stumbled. My nose smacked my father's spine. I steadied myself by pushing off his hips.

"You should've told me that."

It would've been squealing, and Doug had been my friend since freshman year, after they moved next door from Michigan. We'd been teammates. He had been a backup point guard who had a tough time going left. He got sick of getting stripped of the ball during practice and riding the bench during the games, and he quit after junior year. I didn't blame him. If I'd have been a bench ornament, I'd have quit, too.

I almost never sat out. I was a six-four shooting guard averaging twenty-eight a game with letters coming at me from everywhere, including Michigan—places like Ann Arbor, East Lansing, and Kalamazoo. He made me show him all the Michigan letters. Doug said if he was me, he'd go there, even to Kalamazoo. It wasn't so far from Grand Rapids, which is where they used to live when things had been okay. Back then, his father had seemed like other men.

For the last month Doug had been real upset because his father had come out of the closet. He had this young boyfriend he was planning to move in with. He'd been hoping to make it a smooth transition and wanted his wife and son to work through the transition in counseling. Mr. White, Dad had said, had made the mistake of thinking he could blow up the world and have it too. It was a big mistake, Dad had said, to expect everybody to be reasonable.

"I didn't think he'd do it," I shouted. We were crunching across the driveway pebbles. Barney and Andy were way behind, hauling up the hill, guns drawn. "I figured Doug was just mad. People get mad and say, 'I'd like to get a gun.' I figured it was just talk. Maybe he didn't get one."

"Maybe."

We jumped Mrs. White's flowerbed and skidded up the flagstone walk.

My father barged right through the door, no knocking. A gun went off.

"Get down!" he yelled and dropped below the three steps that led up to the living room. I panicked and belly-flopped, catching my chin on the bottom step. Fortunately, the Whites had carpet.

My father inched his eyes over the top step, looked around, and popped up. I crawled up the steps on all fours. The living room was trashed like one of those poltergeist scenes with the whirling shiny spooks tossing newspapers and chairs and pictures and lamps. The sofa was on its back. A potted palm was turned over. Mrs. White was huddled next to the fireplace. Her hands held the sides of her face and her mouth was an oval. Like she'd been flash frozen in place by one of the poltergeists.

"Where are they?" Dad asked.

Mrs. White didn't answer. She seemed to look right through Dad. There was another shot from upstairs.

My father glared at me. "You wait here!"

He bolted up the steps.

Barney and Andy banged on in. Barney—the skinny one—yelled through static. "This is a Code 8. We've got a 10-57 in progress. Repeat. Code 8. 10-57 in progress."

I found Dad and followed him down the long hallway, toward the shouting voices coming from the master bedroom.

Dad tried the knob, but it was locked.

"Doug! Jerry!" he called. "This has gone too far. Time to call it quits."

My father turned. His eyes were ice.

"I thought I told you to wait downstairs."

The gun went off again, real loud. The wall to my left shook, and Dad and I hit the deck. A noise came from behind, and I squirreled around to see Barney and Andy, face down, motioning us to get away. "Ted! Go downstairs." Dad's voice was calm but mean. Ice and fire.

"Doug shot the wall," I said. "He doesn't want to shoot us. If he did, he could've gotten us through the door. We were sitting ducks."

"Please go back down!"

"Doug's my best friend. I know him. He'll listen to me."

God knows what got into me, probably too many movies, but I pushed up from the floor and put my size thirteen Air Jordan's right through the lock. The door flew back, and I stepped in. My father grabbed me and pulled me to the ground, just as the gun went off and a shot whistled past. Dad came down on top of me as Doug fired again. Maybe I didn't know Doug after all.

"Don't move or you guys'll get it, too!" Doug said.

He was on the far side of the bed with a pistol in each hand.

"Calm down, Doug!" my father said. He stood real slow, hands raised in front of him.

Doug pointed his gun at us. "Back against the wall."

My father eased back to the wall, dragging me by the collar. This time, I didn't fight him. I had known enough to kick open the door, but now that I was in the room, I was pretty much out of ideas.

"Okay," Doug said. "Leave."

"Ted'll leave," my father said. "I'm staying."

"Me, too. Doug, you'll have to shoot us."

"I'm thinking about it. For now, just close the damn door."

I got on all fours, crawled to the door, and banged it shut. The cops were on their bellies, inching our way.

"Tom! Ted! You fellas all right?"

It was Mr. White. He was in the bathroom. The door had two bullet holes and two dents near the lock. Two things Doug couldn't do—go left and kick open doors. He was a little guy. Me, I'd have kicked in the door like nothing.

"We're okay," my father told him. "Jerry, I think it's time we all relaxed. This is not the way to settle things."

"I agree!" Mr. White hollered.

Doug fired another shot at the door. "You go to hell!" he screamed.

"Let's talk about this," Dad said. "Tell me what the problem is."

"You wouldn't understand. Your father isn't a fag. Faggot!" he yelled and fired again.

"Jerry! You hanging in there?"

There was no answer.

"Jerry, say something!"

"Hey!" Doug said. "Maybe I got him." He seemed surprised and scared, his voice fluttery. "But I might've only winged him."

He fired again and again. When the bullets were gone, he flung it against the bathroom door. Then he switched the other gun to his right hand. Keeping it pointed at us, he went over to the bathroom door and kicked it, once, twice. Nothing happened. Doug wasn't Tom Cruise or Bruce Willis. He wasn't even Ted Starling.

"Are you alive or dead, you queer?" Doug looked at us. "He hates being called queer. Downstairs I knocked out three of his teeth. Queer! Fag!" Doug kicked the door some more. He wasn't getting anywhere. The dope was kicking with his toe, not his heel. Doug backed off and sat in a padded chair next to the walk-in closet. Pointing the gun at us, he smiled. "He must be dead. I killed my father."

I didn't think Doug would shoot us, but I also hadn't thought he'd kill his father. "Kill" had been just one of those words—the way people talked. *I could've killed him.* In basketball, I talked all the time about killing the other team. A little while ago, my father had talked about killing Allen Iverson because he took too many shots. *I could just kill that guy.* It was only talk, like *how's the weather?* Looking at the gun, I realized we were dealing with another kind of talk. In this room, *I killed my father* meant something. Maybe it meant Doug had gone temporarily insane. But I wondered, could he be temporarily insane and still have gone to the trouble of getting two guns?

"Why don't you let me go in there and take a look at him?" Dad said. "He may be basted not wasted. He may still need to be properly greased."

I almost laughed. This sounded like movie talk. Vietnam movie talk, though my father never went to see them. He made fun of the titles. He'd go on about how *Platoon Balloon* or *Heavy Metal Jacket* or *Apocalypse Last Friday* couldn't be anything like the real thing. They'd be doing their filming on the beach or inside a car wash, while he and his guys would be out on recon, slopping around in the rain.

"What do you mean?" Doug asked.

"I mean, he might not be dead."

"Oh, he's dead, all right. Otherwise, we'd hear him."

"I got big feet," I said. "Let me look. I'll kick the door open."

There was a light tap on the bedroom door.

"Doug White! You're under arrest." It was Barney Fife. His voice was all shaky. "Any minute now, the SWAT team'll be coming through the windows. This is your last chance to come out of this alive."

Doug shot the door. Dad and I ducked. Splinters flew. I heard scurry-scuffling in the hall and "Ouch! Son of a bitch!"

I started to get up. "Ted, stay put!" Dad ordered. To Doug he said, "I can get the door open in no time. What do you say? Why not let me have a look? We've always been pals."

Doug was looking back and forth, scared or crazy or both. He was probably worried, like I was worried, that the SWAT team would be flying through the windows. In a movie I saw, they came right through the walls. Things were happening outside. Sirens were wailing and now all these red lights were showing up. The world outside the window was nothing but swirls and flashes.

Dad was getting up.

"Mr. Starling, you stay put. Ted wanted to do it, so he gets to do it."

"I'll make a deal with you." This is the only time my father sounded even a little scared. He didn't want me to kick open the door and look. "Let Ted kick open the door and then you and me—we'll go inside and have a look."

"No, Ted and I will look. We're teammates aren't we, Ted?"

Doug *was* crazy.

"Sure we are. You should be starting, too. Me and you in the back court. Coach Shuster doesn't know squat."

Doug laughed. "That's right. I'm starting next game. Let's go. Get over here and kick!"

I got up, went to the door, got the knob flush with my heel, and let fly with my big right foot, one of those straight-out jobs where you extend the muscles and yell like those karate guys. "Kiai!" The door snapped back. Before I knew it, my father was there, jerking me away by my neck.

Doug yelled, "Back! Get back!"

The front bedroom window was splashed with a searchlight, and we heard this real calm voice come over a loudspeaker.

"Doug, buddy, time to come out now. It's late and everybody wants to go home to sleep."

"Mr. Starling get back to the other wall! I'm going in there and see if he needs finishing off."

"Tom! Ted! You guys all right? Say something!"

I was shocked. Mr. White was out there on the loudspeaker. Doug looked weird. His head was flapping back and forth.

My father went into the bathroom. When he came out he looked at me.

"There's a little window in the back. He must've shimmied through somehow. I suppose he jumped."

I started in to have a look, but Doug pointed the gun at me. I went back to the wall.

"Are you guys all right?" Mr. White called. His voice crackled over the loudspeaker

Doug fired a shot out the window. "Fag!"

People outside yelled and screamed. Above them all, in a high pitch, I heard Alice wail.

"Doug just killed Teddy!"

"No, he didn't," I shouted. "I'm here and Dad's here. Just don't nobody shoot!"

"Shut up!" Doug ordered. "You sound like a pussy."

My father was standing at the foot of the bed.

"Looks like you missed him. Better luck next time. Now, why don't you hand over that thing, so we can all go downstairs and work on that living room?" He grinned. "It'll take till midnight to find the couch." My father reached out his hand. "Why don't you give me the gun?"

Right then Doug did something that took my breath away. He put the nose of the gun to his right temple.

"I missed part one, but you'll get to see part two. Up close and personal."

The F.M. radio voice was back on the loudspeaker.

"Dougie, boy, this is just a misunderstanding. You're making everything more confusing for everybody. So far, no harm's been done. What we all need to do is sit around the kitchen table and hash this thing out. Like adults. Just in case you're concerned, we're not viewing this as a hostage situation. We're calling this a little misunderstanding."

My father knew all about guns and "nervous nellies." He walked to the window and called out, "This is Tom Starling. I want everybody out there to relax."

I heard my mother's and sisters' screams.

Dad called out the window, and the screaming gagged off into faraway whimpers.

"I think all these police cars and lights and things need to clear the hell out of here. We're not hostages. In fact, Doug's presently got other ideas. He seems to be thinking about making off with himself. It would be best if you'd all let us be."

Now, it was Mrs. White's turn to scream. She flipped the switch and let go with some choking babble. She must've gotten dragged away because the volume got low and muffled.

"You've upset your mother," my father said, turning away. "I think we need to calm her down. You've got responsibilities. How about letting me have the gun?"

Doug took the gun from his head and pointed it at my

father. I could see his finger begin to press. My father's hands went up, and his forehead wrinkled, like he was getting a new idea.

"No!" I screamed in this real squeaky voice. I must've sounded like my sister.

"Ted! Stay cool!" my father ordered.

The calm voice was back on the horn.

"The cars are all gone now. It's time, Doug, for a little chat."

The flashing lights *were* gone.

"Shut up down there!" my father yelled. "I'm busy."

"Doug, he's my father." I was bawling, sniffling like a baby. "Kill your own damn father but leave mine alone!"

The snot was all gluey in my nose. I couldn't breathe through my swollen throat.

"Take it easy, Ted," my father said. "Nothing like that's going to happen. Now, Doug, I want you to think of something. When I was in 'Nam, I went into a tunnel and found myself face to face with a gun. It was one of our own M-16s. Captured, I might add. Charlie pulled the trigger and the gun jammed. Before I could free my arm and toast him, he was gone. I crawled on through, blew up the hole, and figured I was charmed. I did a lot of crazy things and never got scratched. Now what I want to know is, are you going to do what Charlie didn't?"

Doug actually shivered. The gun drooped. But in no time, he had it snug to the side of his head.

"Mr. Starling, I can't stand it. One guy at school said I got born out of my father's asshole. Another guy said being a fag's hereditary. I can get married all I want and have kids and all that, but one day I'll wake up and be queer. I'll come out of the closet, like Dad did. I don't want"—Doug looked like he was going to cry—"to be like that."

"That's just talk," my father said. "Empty talk. Those guys are giving you the business. They smell a certain weakness and then *bam*! Guys used to needle me all the time because I was pin-toed. They said I looked like a pigeon trying to trip over its own feet. When I was seven or eight, I couldn't talk right. The words came out all messed up. This big fat kid next door—he was ten or eleven—used to call me 'Mouthful of Stewed Tomatoes.' Like it was my name. The words always hurt. You have to accept the fact that people will talk. But it's only talk."

I didn't know where Dad was getting this stuff. He wasn't pin-toed, and I'd never heard a thing about his mushy mouth.

"Having a father like I got," Doug said, "is more than talk. He's moving out to live with this twenty-five-year-old fairy. Dad's probably got AIDS. Queers get AIDS."

"Things have changed and people aren't getting AIDS so much anymore, but you never know. Why don't you stick around and see what's going to happen. Maybe he'll get sick in other ways. You never know. You need to be around and see what happens. Shooting him's not what you want to do. Being shot's not so bad. It's quick, except for the ones left behind. But it's easy on the spirit. I've watched guys die from gunshots. They get real cold and drift off to sleep."

"That's why I'm going this way." Doug tapped the side of his head with the gun. "It'll be easy on my spirit."

My father gulped. He realized he'd made a mistake.

"The big thing is, you'd let your father off the hook. You should give yourself another chance and maybe you'll find that there are other things you can do."

Doug laughed. "After this, he won't let me get near him."

"I think he will."

Doug laughed again. "He's not that stupid."

"Sure, he is. Fathers can be fools. If you give it a little time, he'll think you got it out of your system. The best thing to do is to let a little time go by. It'll lull him. He'll get this idea that you've forgiven him. He'll have the crazy thought that you've adjusted."

Doug smiled. "You think that's the way to go?"

"Absolutely. See what happens. Live to see what happens and then you can act accordingly."

"I like that. I can act accordingly. While I'm at it, maybe I can think of something good for Wayne. Wayne's a major problem here. I can think about that while I'm at it."

Doug tossed the gun on the bed. It bounced. Rather than snatching it up, like I wanted to, my father just looked at it with sad, faraway eyes. I would've grabbed the gun myself, except my father started talking weird.

"Look at it this way. Waiting for your chance is a better life than death. The thought of killing your father—people shut it up inside themselves, but it's something to look forward to, plan for. I've done it myself a million times."

Dad must've been blowing more smoke. What I'm saying is, he didn't have a father around to kill. My grandfather died when my father was eleven or twelve. I don't know what he died of. When I'd ask about it, my father always said, "He just died." And my mother said, "Don't ask. He'll tell you someday." They were both weird about it, so I stopped asking.

Dad has this little wooden box with about twenty black and white and color pictures of him and his father. He keeps the box in the top of his bedroom closet. He showed the pictures to me once. They were simple shots—the two of them with baseballs and bats and footballs. They'd be at the park or on the beach. That kind of stuff. There was nothing in any of them to give you the idea of murder. There was nothing strange about any of them, except once, through a crack in the bedroom door, I caught sight of my father sitting on the bed, the box in his lap, and all these pictures spread out over the blanket like cards. They were laid out like he was playing solitaire. And he was just staring at them without moving. He didn't look like he wanted to kill anything. He only looked like he couldn't move.

HOUSE ARREST

For the second morning in a row, from his sister's screened side porch, Hedge watched them round the corner on their crooked noisy march to the bus stop, those teenage goofs with their funny hair—greased-up spikes sticking straight up, razor-shaved bald around the sides, draggle-tailed tufts fluttering below their necks.

It irritated Hedge; they were out, and he was in.

Hugging himself, Hedge rocked back from the table and spied the perfect perch: what a gas it would be to sit up on that limb and fire a few warning rounds at their feet. A little dancing dust to make the Stooges bolt.

There was Moe, stomping the skateboard like a mini teeter-totter, clack and clack, flopping edge to edge in a fitful travesty of forward motion. Occasionally, as he stumbled, Moe hefted his weight and let the board glide in swooping circles and half-moon arcs, dipping low, not quite wiping out but wrenching out of his loop to clack back into his skateboard strut. Right behind him, lumpy Larry plodded, shouldering a boom box the size of a small trunk. From the speakers blasted a percussive assault—guitar strangulation and vocal slaughter, the heavy metal wreck of suicide music. It reminded Hedge of the tent wars back in 'Nam—the humping shelling of Motown jamming in a kickass firefight with the psycho-ricochet of Hendrix. Nobody cared. If you needed sleep, you slept. When you were awake, the tent wars helped: canned thunder crowded out The Fear. Currently in Brookfield, there was nothing to fear. There were only pests—the encroachment of industrial parks, the threat of luxury taxes, the slumping financial markets, the behavior of the neighborhood kids, smart-assed happy pests bopping through the streets at 7:13 a.m.

In rehab, Hedge had become an early riser. It was one of the new fundamentals for making himself presentable. For some time (How long depended on what you wanted to count. The spasmodic excesses of his final spree? Or the accretion of lamentable episodes?) Hedge had been very unpresentable, a husband enraged with his wife, a father disgusted with his children, a war hero fed up with his country. Rising early made him work at enjoying life, to not expect too much, to tolerate boredom as well as pests. At least the Stooges were using up a good four minutes of his sentence.

Now take Curly, Hedge mused. Curly was about as diverting as a poorly trained seal, nimble but not nimble enough. In his baggy flowery shorts, Curly danced in the street, a human pogo stick, hopping on his left foot while his right foot tickled the air. From afar, he seemed to be poking his toe at nothing. Up close, just beyond the property line, the bit of nothing assumed shaped. Curly was kicking a hacky sack. Hedge's boy had one. Neither bag nor ball, it resembled a lumpy pincushion. It didn't bounce and wasn't worth throwing. You couldn't serve, bat, or putt it. You could only dance with it.

"Somebody ought to do something about them."

Hedge turned. His sister, Sharon Morgan, dressed in a long white silk robe, stood in the doorway that opened into the dining room. She was raking her short straight black hair with a blue towel. In family photos, Hedge and his sister were often mistaken for twins.

"I can't stand the noise. It flat-out isn't right." Hedge smiled: with the Stooges to pick at, maybe Sharon would let him slide. "I mean, what if you had a baby sick, or you worked nights?"

"Nobody in this neighborhood works nights," Hedge replied mildly. "This place is strictly nine to four." By now, the heavy metal screed was fading away, a gnarled declension into nada.

"That's not the point, Al. It's rude—invasive and rude."

Hedge swung his feet over the bench. Leaning forward, he faced Sharon, hands on knees, set, like he was ready to bolt.

"I don't think anyone ever asked them to turn it down. They look like considerate boys to me. They're just a little deaf."

"They're about as considerate as a dust storm."

"If you'd like," Hedge sweetly suggested, "I'll be happy to hash it out with them. I'll invite them to the lawn." Hedge was not allowed to step beyond the Morgan property line. In the penultimate phase of his sentence, he was under house arrest. "I'll put it to them nice."

"I wouldn't do that if I were you. Your time's almost up. Talking to those idiots will only get you excited."

"Excited" was Sharon's word that covered and contained Hedge's wildness. Calm, he was fine—a bit grumpy and sarcastic, somewhat detached, floating out of reach, but fine. Excited, he was a bomb—a testy tank of disruption, volatile, rash, trouble looking for trouble. It was her job, this solid month, to keep her brother calm. So far, Sharon had almost succeeded. Hedge had done his best to be a good boy. After all, if waking up strapped to a hospital bed under armed guard doesn't make you want to be good—well, you might just as soon start a high-speed chase and slam a friendly wall. Get it over with quick and don't take anybody with you.

For kicks, the fat deputy sheriff had pulled his gun, poked the barrel into Hedge's nose, farted real loud and said, "Don't move, Al! You're covered! Get it? Covered!" Hedge was up to his chin with an itchy blanket. He couldn't remember much, just that final blur before the booze and pills socked in: Re Re, his wife, crossing in front of the bedroom TV, taking off her skirt, letting it drop. *Her naked bum startles him: she had blue on when she came out of the shower. She goes shopping and comes home without any drawers.*

"What'd I do?" Hedge had groaned.

Deputy Sheriff Weathers laughed and filled him in.

After breaking Re Re's nose, Hedge had dragged her down the steps. His kids jumped him. Chad, his fourteen-year-old boy, wound up with contusions and a broken arm. Cindy, his eleven-year-old girl, lost a molar. Hedge took off in his Blazer and figured to smash the front door of Tom Meyer's house. Hedge had Meyer pegged as Re Re's lover. The problem was he didn't slam Meyer's house at all. Tom Meyer hadn't even been Re Re's lover. Hedge's boss was. Norm Costello owned the Chevy dealership where Hedge was then service manager. While Costello got off the hook, Meyer's next-door neighbor didn't. It was Pete Macavoy's door that got in Hedge's way. After climbing through the wrecked foyer, Hedge beat Macavoy all over the house.

It took the cops ten minutes to get there—a neighbor 911-ed the crash—and another five to subdue Hedge.

Fortunately for Hedge, who hadn't wanted any help, Herm and Sharon Morgan rode the white horse of One Last Chance. They'd convinced Hedge to not sign or say anything. Sharon said she owed it to her parent's memory to take care of her excitable older brother. The Morgans sprung for one of those expensive, famous lawyers who never totally lose. Soon, two counts each of attempted murder and aggravated assault melted into disorderly conduct. Drug possession became the user-friendly DUI.

In court, Alexander Bartram waved his wand and conducted a symphony. He trundled forth experts on Post Combat Stress Disorder. The jury bought it and the judge levied a contingent sentence: probation under treatment; resentencing if the terms of probation were violated.

Three weeks in Vet detox weaned Hedge from the pills and booze. He then did six weeks in rehab. He gratefully accepted the brainwashing, the body building, the lectures, the films, the books, the counseling, and the art therapy. It was like being in summer camp with a lot of messed-up guys. His day was designed to vanquish idleness and raze the devil's workshop.

The problem was, the devil didn't need a workshop. He only needed a little open space.

"Relax," Hedge smiled. "I was just kidding. I wouldn't bother with them. Maybe somebody should call the cops." He shrugged but couldn't quite bite back that smirking laugh. Something was playing in the devil's amphitheater—Hedge could see himself karate-kicking Moe from the skateboard, smashing Larry's box with a baseball bat, stuffing Curly's hacky sack down his throat.

"You think they're funny," Sharon huffed. "And why not? They're just like you. No respect for anybody."

Hedge frowned sincerely. Sharon was still sore. He had let her down.

"I have respect. I've straightened myself out."

"You were a disgrace. You ruined dinner."

Last night had been Hedge's opportunity to mix with "normal society." The problem was not dinner but the guest list.

Joe Solomon was a blowhard, his wife a worshipful cackler. The third guest was Judy Starnes, a shattered neighbor from two doors down, a rubbery-faced, painted, pushy woman of fifty. Three weeks ago, she had been dumped by her husband of twenty-seven years. From the start, Judy Starnes put him on edge. Flouncing, forward, all touchy-feely, faking light-headedness after three sips of wine, Judy laughed overloud at Solomon's dumb jokes and then draped tickling fingers around Hedge's neck. He started craving a single shot of the Jack.

"It was Solomon's fault. He pushed me."

"It was personally and professionally embarrassing. Utterly offensive."

Joe Solomon was the top producer in Sharon's office. Last year, he managed to unload eight million dollars' worth of overpriced homes.

"I'm sorry, but that 2-S slug acted like he knew about 'Nam."

"So what! He likes to talk. Salesmen talk. You should've just screened it out. I thought you were making progress, but now I'm worried. At the end of next week, you're time's up. I'm afraid you won't be ready."

"I'll be ready. But you gotta see how it rubbed me the wrong way when he said my Silver Star wasn't nearly as good as the Congressional Medal of Honor."

"You need to tolerate what you don't like."

Hedge was grateful when Herm stuck his cheerful, freshly shaven face out the dining room door. Tall and handsome with receding temples and a square jaw, Herm was general manager of the Brookfield Centre Mall.

"I'm firing up the griddle. How about omelets all round?"

Herm's offer was swallowed by silence.

"Hey, if that's a problem, I'll save the cheese and just scramble the suckers."

"Omelets would be wonderful, dear." The starch in Sharon's voice made Hedge itch. "Just give us a few more minutes. We're getting something straight."

"Yeah," Hedge blurted, not sure where it was coming from, "we're reminding me I'm an asshole." Hedge then laughed. Behind his wife's back, Herm winked, gave him one thumb up and pulled his head back into the house.

"It's no joke!" Sharon snarled.

"I know. I'm just admitting the truth."

"You were worse than that."

"So was Solomon! He's the guy doesn't believe in the rehabilitation of criminals. I'm the exception proves the rule."

"He shouldn't have said that."

"He's a Nazi with that stuff about surplus population!"

Hedge had taken it all personally. He couldn't help but see himself as part of the surplus population.

"What he *meant* was we have to take world population seriously. We have limited resources."

"I lost it when he mentioned castration."

"You see this knife?" Hedge screams, hauling back from the table,

standing. "You see this knife?" He machete-slashes the air, grabs the leg of his Cornish hen and buries the knife. "You can't do castration without cutting flesh!" Hedge withdraws the knife and stabs the hen in the back. For emphasis.

"How could we eat after what you did? It was savage."

Hedge stifled a laugh. The jungle dog had surrendered.

"You ruined dinner. After your explosion he hardly said two words."

"I know. We had a nice meal."

During breakfast, Hedge repressed his rage and played the abject sinner—all sorry as hell and swollen with future resolves. Frumpy and imperious, Sharon ate her omelet. Herm worked hard to smooth the wrinkles, covering news, weather, sports, making certain as he patted his lips with a napkin to remind Hedge to fill out that application. Herm had paved the way for Hedge to start right in as assistant service manager at the mall's Sears Auto Center.

When the Morgans left for the day, Hedge was still steaming. They could get the pills and booze out of Hedge, but they couldn't quite get at the rage.

He went to the recreation room and broke into his twirling dance. For a good thirty seconds, Hedge stomped, spun, kicked, and jabbed. One day in group, the guys had all been invited to try Primal Scream Therapy. With frantic joy, they let everything out—aaagh! and aggghhhh! It was fun, this stuff, but it made Hedge feel psycho. It was like running naked in the wind—good for you but dangerous. With the doctor's consent, Hedge substituted his twirling dance.

When he stopped, out of breath, woozy, he didn't want to kill Joe Solomon anymore. Feeling his way up the steps, Hedge went to the kitchen and got a glass of water. It was time to get down to business. Rather than pressing license plates for three cents an hour, Hedge worked around the house. He washed dishes, scraped pots, and scoured pans. He dusted and vacuumed. As he pushed the beater-brush, lifting the nape of the plush cranberry carpet, Hedge carried the cordless phone with him. His probation officer, Ray Raymond, was liable to call at any time. If Hedge didn't pick up the phone, it would be assumed he was out, at large, and in violation of parole. This wasn't baseball. One strike and he was gone.

It helped that Hedge could take the cordless phone outside, where he could be especially useful. Over the last three weeks, he had painted the entire house—two coats of Bohemian Blue—and replaced all the rain gutters. He re-screened the side porch. All this work—it was a new fix.

Hedge spent three hours squatting on his haunches, his back nettled with stickers, knees mud-wet through his work pants. He was behind the shrubs and flower beds, patching cracks in the foundation. Tomorrow he would coat the entire surface with Thompson's WaterSeal. Toward the end of his circuit, while Hedge was leaning way out, doing his best to keep from falling into the azaleas, the cordless phone trilled.

"Morgan residence."

"What're you doing today? Building a marble gazebo?"

It was Ray Raymond. Hedge always felt sorry for people with joke names—Joyce Joyce, Joe Citizen, anybody named Koch, Fuchs, Teeter, or Malarkey.

"I'm plugging cracks. When I'm done, I'll work out."

Ray Raymond sighed. "Hedge, just remember: you're one of the good ones. I only call you up because I have to." Ray Raymond was trying to sucker him. He would call later, maybe many times later. "I'm feeling all let down. One of my first offense rapists is back in the joint. He couldn't resist. The lady was in her eighties. Now tell me, Hedge, what do you make of a guy like that?"

"The usual," Hedge grunted. "It's not supposed to make sense."

He was impatient to get Ray Raymond off the line. Today was the day. After weeks of worrying, Hedge hoped he'd have the guts to make a run for it.

"It's a terrible thing, Hedge, because you find yourself thinking if they're gonna do it, why not go after something nice?"

"Ray, this cement I got on this here trowel is drying out."

Ray Raymond sighed again, like his feelings were hurt. Hedge saw this as just another cop trick.

"Don't go getting mad! I'm just one of the working stiffs. I wanted to catch you once today, just for the record. I probably won't be catching you again for a whole friggin' week."

Hedge smiled: tomorrow he'd have another paintbrush all set. Ray Raymond was going to be dropping by.

Hedge had already done half an hour's time on Sharon's exercise bike and another half hour bouncing on his toes and pounding Herm's punching bag. After five sets of fifty sit-ups, he was now facedown in the backyard, the cordless phone beside him on the grass, finishing his third and final set of push-ups. Lifting himself slowly, his arms quavering, he imagined himself beating back the lactic acid armies swarming in his muscles.

Thirty-seven. "Ugh!" he grunted, sinking slowly, pausing, his arms toned and poised, his lower back straight—no cheating—nose snuffling the grass.

Thirty-eight. Hedged pushed himself up.

On the picnic table, a small portable boom box played Beethoven's *Pastoral*. Hedge was not a classical music buff—in fact, it bored him—but he had discovered in rehab that the musing mix of strings, horns, and winds blowing behind the tinkling piano, and even the rumbling drum, relaxed him.

Thirty-nine. The sound filtered through him without stealing his thoughts. It settled and fixed them. Over the last two hours, Ludwig smoothed some wrinkles in Hedge's soul and helped him make up his mind.

Forty.

Hedge collapsed on the grass, the blades prickling, a cool mat on his whiskered face. As soon as he caught his breath, he really would make a run for it. It would be foolish and risky, but he needed to find something out. He had cased the operation.

The Morgans, as Ray Raymond knew, had call-waiting, so Hedge couldn't simply leave the phone off the hook. There was another way. He would use Ray Raymond against himself. Ray did not like to make a fool of himself in the same way. Once, Ray had gotten all in a lather because the Morgan line had been busy. He came rushing over to find Hedge in the backyard, well within bounds, sitting at the picnic table and shooting the breeze with his sister. Sharon had been on her cell phone, stuck downtown in gridlock. Before she called out of boredom, Hedge had been listening to one of those recorded computer spiels. With Sharon rattling away, Hedge had forgotten to hang up the other line. Ray Raymond acted all embarrassed and apologetic. He figured Hedge jury-rigged the busy signal so he could make a little getaway, which was exactly what he now planned to do.

The cordless phone rang. Languidly, Hedge rolled over on his back, lifted the unit and touched the switch. "Morgan residence," Hedge mumbled in his most gravelly voice.

"Hedge, what's wrong? You having a heart attack?" It was Ray Raymond.

"No such luck. I was taking a nap. I just drifted off."

"Didn't mean to bother you, but I got an idea. A little reward, say. Because you're such a good boy. I just stopped in to see one of my hookers and told her about you. She loves ex-Marines and would be happy to make a free house call. Only thing, Hedge, while you do it, she wants you to wear the top half of your dress regimentals and pay her cab fare."

Hedge jabbed the button, choking off Ray Raymond's horse laugh.

He sat up and stretched his leg muscles. He flicked on the phone and sprinted toward the back of the lot. Hedge leaped over the line. On his heels, he skidded down a crumbling hill, the pebbles rolling beneath his sneakers. He raced along a winding path cluttered with logs and dead leaves, ducking under outstretched limbs, twisting away from grappling vines. He bounced across the rocks of a small stream and stumbled up the embankment. Fifty yards ahead, there was sunlight. Soon, he skittered to the rutted shoulder of County Lane.

As he pounded toward the Exxon sign, skipping over shards of glass and peeled tires, the ground crackled and gave way. Sliding to a stop, he raked two quarters from the back pocket of his gray sweatpants. Hedge stepped beneath the public phone's cracked plastic dome, lifted the receiver, dropped in the coins, and poked out the Morgan number. With the phone ringing, Hedge set the receiver on the torn, open pages of the phone book and then jogged the next hundred yards. He reserved the last thirty for his cool-down walk.

He wiped his face with the belly of his green T-shirt. He finger-combed his short black hair. With his breathing only slightly rushed, he pulled the heavy iron door and stepped inside Roadside Roy's cool afternoon night. The bartender—a bald, fat man with a gray paintbrush mustache—stood at the far end of the bar. He rested one foot on the ledge of the lower sink, his head tilted back, staring at a stock-car race playing on the overhead screen. A young man in blue work clothes sat at the middle of the bar, hunched over a sandwich and a glass of beer. He didn't even look up. That Hedge had arrived was no big deal. Fighting bank-robber nervousness, Hedge stood behind one of those old-fashioned stools with the red vinyl seats, silver studded stitching and no backs. The bartender waddled Hedge's way.

"What do ya say, pal?"

"I'll have a Black Jack on the rocks. You still got a phone?"

The bartender pointed with his chin. At the end of a short corridor, the Gents door on his left, the Gals door on his right, Hedge grabbed the receiver, fumbled out two quarters and punched in the numbers.

"It's busy!" Hedge said, looking into the graffiti scrawl. The beep-beep-beep amazed him. Usually, his plans didn't work.

With relief, Hedge went back to his place. Standing behind his stool, his fingers lifting the sweating glass, his heart twisting with dread, Hedge sipped the whiskey. It sloshed around his teeth and went down. He did not turn into a bat or sprout fangs. He took a longer pull, surprised, disturbed—no, pleased. The booze burned his throat and stomach. Again he sipped, relieved: he didn't really want it. He had been right: throughout all the hours of counseling and confession, all the I'm-really-bad admissions, Hedge had never considered himself to be an alcoholic, a problem drinker, yes, but not an alcoholic. Even with his body twisting in the wrench of withdrawal, even during those days when he wet his lips and longed. Not that he could tell anybody.

These days, everybody was schooled in the dynamics of denial. All Hedge could do was bide his time and prove it to himself, away. Of course, Sharon kept booze in the house, but he was sure she had every drop measured. So he forged his own plan. He went out and now he would go back. He would not take one for the road.

The cubes rattled. Hedge left a six-dollar tip. During his return run, his stomach feeling sick, he hung up the public phone like a good citizen. Behind the Morgan line, he slipped going up the hill, banging his knee on a boulder. But the pain tasted great. Knowing when it hurt was normal. He tripped crossing the property line and sprinted the final stretch. With a pronounced stroke, he turned off the cordless phone. Winded, he dropped down and rolled over. The white clouds humped and twisted into feathery horses leaping above the shifting trees.

Having sold a three bedroom for four hundred thousand, Sharon arrived home in a lilting mood. She smooched and tickled Herm. She rubbed Hedge's face and poked him in the ribs. "It's so wonderful to come home to two handsome men!"

The two handsome men smiled uncomfortably. Flirtation did not sit well on Sharon.

"Since I'm today's big breadwinner, I'll leave it to you guys to take over the kitchen." The two guys almost always took over the kitchen. "I'm going to the club for a swim and a sauna."

One of the things Hedge liked about Herm was his shrugging indifference to money. That Sharon had scored sixteen thousand in commission and fees was no big deal to him.

In the kitchen, while the men prepared dinner—veal Oscar, sweet potatoes, asparagus, Greek salad—Herm was far more interested in discussing his latest brainstorm, an All-Mall Weekday Walking Workout for Senior Citizens. That afternoon, he had gotten it organized, even down to the posters and newspaper and radio promotions.

"It'll encourage the oldsters to get in shape. *Registered* oldsters will get an extra five percent off all non-sale items. In all stores. On Monday we'll have a ribbon cutting and everything. The Mayor will be there. We'll have balloons. I even dug up this senior citizen marching band. The merchants'll love it."

Throughout dinner, Sharon went out of her way to be nice.

"Al, I simply love the job you did covering those ugly cracks. You really shouldn't have gone to so much trouble."

"The way I see it—you move or die. Like Herm's walk for the old bags."

"Speaking of moving," Herm piped up. "Sharon and I would like you to forget about moving out. When your time's up, we want you to stay with us. You can save money and get back on your feet. You and me—we can even carpool."

"Carpool" was Herm's tactful way of addressing Hedge's transportation woes. His license was suspended for another three months. Even then it wouldn't matter. Hedge transcended the Assigned Risk category. In the car insurance world, he was to safe driving what junk bonds were to fiscal responsibility.

"I'll find an apartment and walk to work. I'm in the way here."

"That's ridiculous," Sharon said. "Besides, you really do need to save your money."

"It won't matter," Hedge moaned. "Whatever I make, they're gonna take."

Herm waved these mournful thoughts away. "That's why there are lawyers in the world. She can't get it all." Herm and Sharon were also springing for Hedge's divorce lawyer. "You'll be surprised by what Marv Ziner will be able to salvage. He's a magical man."

Hedge nodded and got up. He didn't even want to think about the figures in Pete Macavoy's civil suit. After dinner, it was his habit to retreat to his room and stay there till eleven. Herm and Sharon needed their own life. Hedge needed to feed his latest addiction.

Herm owned all of John Le Carre's books. During the day and in the evenings, Hedge had been consuming them in chronological order. Certain scenes, his favorite characters, had become like memory bytes of his own life. It shook him up when Alec Leamas got shot to pieces after vacillating atop the Berlin Wall and then climbing back down. All for Liz, who was already wasted. Smiley was down there, on the western side, calling for Hedge to jump. Now Smiley—there was a good guy with his own troubles. His wife slept around and it took him forever to catch Karla. They were all part of Hedge's squad. Magnus Pym—another joke name—let his father swallow his life, and don't forget poor Jerry Westerby, who called everybody "sport." He, too, took it for Liz, a different Liz. Hedge detected a pattern. Maybe Le Carre—his real name was David something—got burned by someone named Liz.

Hedge closed the bedroom door. It clicked behind him. On the nightstand pile was *The Russia House*. He started right in, curious to see what old Dave was going to do after they took the Cold War away. But he couldn't leap the divide. Instead, he was floating above the abyss, looking for a soft place to land. He was wondering about making another run. But first he would reconnoiter.

Against everyone's advice, against the law, in violation of parole, Hedge picked up the phone and punched in the number. His daughter, Cindy, answered.

"Hello." Heavy metal music clanked in the background.

In a graveled, grating voice, Hedge asked for an old friend.

"May I talk to Sergeant Al Hedge?"

She paused, suspicious, and then blurted, "Daddy doesn't live here anymore. Who are you?"

A good question! Hedge's mind reeled. Instinctively, he plucked a joke name.

"I'm Joe. Joe Joseph. An army pal. One of the guys your father saved."

"Mom says, 'That's the only decent thing he ever did, but stick around awhile, it'll turn out he saved a serial killer.' We all hate Daddy."

"I'm not a killer, Cindy."

"How'd you know my name?"

Hedge wavered in the vertigo of improvisation.

"I remember when you were born. Your father sent me a card. Since then I turned over a new leaf. I've become a priest. Now I'm Father Joseph Joseph."

Cindy laughed. "That's a funny name."

"My parents were in love with St. Joseph."

"Who's he?"

"A very trusting husband."

"Cool. How was he trusting?"

Hedge was running out of ideas, and Cindy was bored.

"It's a long story. Ask your Daddy. While you're at it, tell him Joe Joseph called."

"I'll get Mommy to tell the lawyer. We never talk to Daddy. There's a court order. Mom says he's criminally insane and should be breaking rocks in the hot sun. He got off the hook for trying to kill everybody. He's at his sister's house. Mom says they're all over there laughing at the court."

"I'm sure nobody's laughing. Well, Cindy, don't forget to tell your mother I called." Hedge took a flyer. "Or maybe I could say a word to her myself."

With a little prayer to St. Joseph, Hedge decided to reveal himself. He'd tell Re Re he had changed. He'd say, "That guy who floored you—it wasn't me."

"She ain't here now. She's out with Norm. He's awesome. He bought me the new PlayStation and he gets me any game I want. Norm lives here now. As soon as Mommy's divorce goes through, they're gonna get married. Then I'll be rich. Hey, you're a priest! Maybe you can marry them."

Hedge cleared his throat. "That's nice of you to ask, but I simply won't be able to. You see, I'm calling long distance." Hedge thought of faraway places. The Pitcairn Islands. Madagascar. The melting Antarctic shelf. "Right now I'm in Tacoma. In seven days, I leave for Tibet. I'm going to work on converting Buddhist monks. Back in the war, they used to light themselves on fire."

"Whatever. Well, have fun. I'll tell Mom you called."

"Please do and tell her I'll say a prayer for your father."

"The hell with him! The bastard chipped my tooth."

Reading was out. Hedge opened the window and stepped out to the slanting roof, careful to keep his footing on the slippery shingles. He settled slowly into place, resting his back on the freshly painted shakes. With his hands cupped around his knees, his head touching the wall, he looked beyond the stunted evergreens to the evening lights of nearby houses. Normal adults were watching TV, helping kids with homework, getting ready to call it a day. Sitting on the roof, alone in the chill of his private Tibet, Hedge imagined sliding to the garage roof and jumping to the grass. He wondered what it would be like to slip slowly off, to go outside like any other person who needed to walk off the woes of the day, move or die, then come back, not to a halfway house, but to a home.

The shingles scratched Hedge's behind. He shifted his weight. He wasn't going anywhere. Soon he would crawl back in, give old Le Carre another go, figure out what was happening at the Moscow book fair and try to get lost on the trails of international intrigue. There he might forget he had a daughter, a son, a wife, and that they all hated him. When he found his way out, maybe he could remember that today he had proven himself normal, that he only had seven more days on the inside, that he could then travel at-large, carry the weight of his balance, and try to find his way past the invisible moving wall.

MULEKICK

I don't know how it is exactly, but sometimes fifteen minutes turns into twenty years.

The gray bearded priest with the lavender vestments held the big book and recited words from many different pages. For the infant, there were prayers of welcome, thanksgiving, and hope. They weren't so bad. After all, that's what a baby is—the freshest of starts, the universe's next genius—pure possibility squirming and grunting in a crinkling diaper. But let's face it: Hitler, Dahmer, and the rest of the killers had all been babies. I'm sure they coo-cooed and gurgled with the best of them. That's the trouble with pure possibility. Things generally slide in the other direction. If grown-up babies don't often achieve the magnitude of mass slaughter, they do get tangled in the everyday malaise. I'm counting myself in this, even though I lived in Hollywood and wrote for one of the more successful soaps. People thought I led an exciting life, but I didn't. My dullness simply included worse traffic jams and frequent poolside parties. Don't get me wrong: I loved my only nephew, soon to be my godson, but I didn't know much about him. No one did. How did I know he wouldn't turn into a mean son-of-a-bitch? I didn't, couldn't.

The prayers for adults really slowed down time. First, we renounced Satan and all his snares. Then Father Stubbings offered prayers of obeisance, penitence, and supplication. With extended hands, he invited us to lapse into silence and make wishes. We had seven-and-a-half years to beg for new cars, better looks, miracle cures, and winning lottery tickets. I concocted my vision of happiness: paradise in the form of an unpolluted beach with a spacious cabana, a new wife at least marginally compatible, and leisure to read and then re-read all the novels ever written by Charles Dickens. Not that reading *Little Dorrit* would help me write better scripts. Applying Dickens would only make them worse. It's just too bad that moral resolution and narrative closure have so little to do with life on the post-contemporary tundra.

"Now, I will anoint young Thomas John with the Oil of the Communicants, one of the sacred oils of the church. The sign of our Savior's cross signifies this child's entry into Christian trial and redemption."

Linda Elmore sniffed, maybe by accident. She was standing next to me and was the godmother, the only sister of Peter, my brother-in-law. He was a thin nervous man with round shoulders and a slithery walk. He was circulating on the edges, making everybody nervous with that mini-cam. When the priest came over, Linda stiffened, as if waiting to be slapped. When she hefted the baby up her thin chest, you'd have thought she was handling a bug-infested log. Father Stubbings smeared a greasy cross on the kid's blotched forehead and stained the satin cap. Linda grimaced. At the house, before we came over, she had barked about paying forty bucks for the outfit. Thomas John didn't like the way things were going, either. He kicked and writhed. Linda I didn't care about, but I felt for the baby. He couldn't have been comfortable swaddled inside those eighteen layers of satin. Like his godfather, I'm sure he wanted to get the hell away.

Through a long snowy winter, we recited the Lord's Prayer. I moved my lips, played with my fingers, and observed the mumbling crowd of thirty or so, mostly the married friends of Loni and Peter. There were a lot of strange children, no eligible women and a single decrepit, aging cousin we called Uncle Billy. He was propped up on metal crutches.

Outside the church, before the ceremony, while we had huddled and sweated in the broiling sun, Uncle Billy had given my left shin a knock.

"Hey, Dave, I just found out we don't gotta sit through Mass."

He meant we just had to get through the Baptismal rite and then scoot back for the eats and drinks.

I shrugged and sighed. "Loni told me I had to be ready for Mass. It's one of the reasons I promised to go to confession. So I could take Communion and not embarrass her."

"Don't worry," he cackled. "They do Communion at these jobs. I just don't know when."

We did it right after the Lord's Prayer.

Father Stubbings trudged to the tabernacle and took out a gold chalice filled with wafers. He stomped back and held one to Linda's face. She fused her lips and went, "Uh-uh."

Linda was an atheist—the atheist godmother—but she was there anyway, hating every minute of it. Don't ask me why. I was (had been?—am?—I don't know what) a Catholic, but had totally fallen away. In some dim part of me, I still believed something, though I didn't know what. Since at least one godparent had to be a Catholic in good-standing, I had succumbed to the pressures of sibling love and made the great sacrifice: I got reconciled. Fortunately, after asking around, I found a radical priest chilling out in a run-down parish two blocks east of Hollywood Boulevard. Late last Saturday, I went to confession. I was surprised: they no longer make you kneel inside a box and whisper to a shadow behind a screen. Now they let you humiliate yourself face to face. I went into a small room with two wooden armchairs, a ratty rug, and a vivid painting of the murdered Jesus. It was like a job interview. Waiting for me was a bald, ex-hippie priest with long straggly side-hair and a walrus mustache. I had never forgotten the introductory lines.

"Bless me, Father, for I have sinned. It's been twenty-seven years since my last confession."

His eyes lighted and he smirked. Tonight he'd have a real sinner.

"What brings you back to our Holy Mother, the church?"

I told him and he grinned.

"Do you come back to us with an open heart and a true desire for reconciliation?"

I took this as sarcasm.

"I certainly do," I said. "I'm here to confess my sins. I can be general or specific. Whatever you prefer."

"Be as specific as you like."

He was leaning forward, all ears, as if I were about to tell dirty jokes. In a manner of speaking, I did. Forty-five minutes later, we agreed I had consistently committed all Seven Deadly Sins but intermittently violated only seven of the Ten Commandments—murder, theft, and overt dishonor to my parents being foreign to my nature. Father Donadio absolved me in the name of God and gave me a difficult penance: "Try to stay out of jams, especially ones that violate the sanctity of the flesh." I agreed to try.

The following Monday, I dropped into the rectory and filled out a parish registration form. On Wednesday, I picked up my stamped, signed, and sealed certificate of good standing. Next day, before I left for the airport and my flight east, I checked my mail and found a three months' supply of collection envelopes.

"Body of Christ!" Father Stubbings proclaimed.

"Amen," I replied.

The Savior's wholeness settled and dissolved on the parched porch of my tongue.

It took a solid year for the crowd to take Communion, and before I knew it, fall turned to winter and winter came back to spring, and here we were at the baptismal font, a green marble basin three feet deep, four feet in diameter. It looked like a Jacuzzi for sacred midgets, this tub of gently circulating holy water. The priest held a gold scooper and asked Linda to extend Thomas John above the waters of life. She struggled to get his cap off, tossed it at me, and with quaking arms, she held him out. The priest slowly baptized him in the name of the Father, the Son, and the Holy Ghost. For each person of the Trinity, he scooped a whole ladle of holy water. On the third pour, the baby jerked around, gushed a mouthful of puke on to Linda's throat, and then screeched and kicked. Linda panicked. Her mouth wobbled and her head bobbed. Lumpy chunks dropped inside her dress.

"Take him! Take him!" she hissed. I hunched forward, bumped a tall candle, and slipped my hand under the satin swaddle. I brought him back to my chest, away from the basin. I had a better grip on the clothes than on the child. When Thomas John spit up in my face, I flinched and gagged. He wrenched and spun, turned once and tumbled. With my heart seized, I stabbed my hand through air clotted with sudden cries and gasps. I snagged a foot and pulled. He swung back and forth, wailing, in metronomic motion, grotesquely resembling those movie moments of upside-down birth. He then slithered out of his satin bootie and fell. With a deft soccer-style kick, I shoveled him sideways. He just made it over the basin and splashed, achieving total immersion.

Loni shoved the startled priest, plunged her hands into the water, and gathered her choking, dripping, hysterical darling to the safety of her non-lactating breasts. The baby sputtered and gasped. My knees wobbled. The room tilted. I smothered in a rapid strangle, the near swoon of merely averted disaster.

Back at Loni's house, at the edge of an elaborate buffet spread beneath the center of a rented backyard tent, I ate five deviled eggs and four rolls: the awful yoke, mustard, and mayonnaise fluff was gastronomic penance. I wolfed it all down in hopes that gobs of egg and stale dough would soak up my third double bourbon. I hadn't intended to drink—I almost never drink before evening—but I was trying to neutralize the radiating ostracism. I was breathing it, the fumes of my expulsion: I was not the hero who had saved the baby, but the villain who almost killed and then kicked him. I'd been at the party for nearly two hours and no one wanted to talk to me. When I angled into conversational circles, talk sagged and people slinked away. It was Loni's fault, actually. They were taking sides with her. In church she had called me a dumb ass—an irresponsible, obnoxious, self-absorbed child-killer. I was "as bad as Herod's soldiers." She'd actually said that. If I lived to be a thousand, she'd screamed, she never wanted to speak to me again. She was going to have my godfathership annulled. There was more, but you get the drift. By the time Loni got home, she had simmered into a kind of murderous politeness, a cold-smile stare that said I belonged in hell. Only Uncle Billy wanted anything to do with me.

Soon after Loni went into the house with the baby, he whacked my shin with his crutch.

"That was some stunt. I thought for a second we'd be into some serious brain damage. That floor's marble. Did your mother ever tell you about this kid we knew growing up? He'd be a man now, unless he's dead, but he was four, see, and one day he got up fast under a table and cracked open his skull. Pip was the name. At least that's what we called him. He never got mentally older than seven or so. But he was one happy son-of-a-bitch. It's a friggin' lesson in life. He could only get jobs that—"

I broke loose and went off to kill a few conversations. I finally got the message and staked out turf by the buffet. You're probably wondering why I came back to the party at all. Linda certainly hadn't come back. If I could've gone home, just taken a hike, I might've left. But my stuff was up in the guest room. My return ticket was for Thursday. It couldn't be changed without hundreds in penalties. Even with what I make, I wasn't interested in paying full coach fare. A one-way ticket—I did make a call—with a five p.m. departure from Newark International cost more than my round trip ticket. You figure it out. But this is by the way. The real reason I didn't bolt—who needs a dull afternoon party, et cetera, et cetera?—was because I didn't want to lose Loni, my only sibling. I needed to stick around and make up. By the end of the day, maybe she'd get used to me almost killing her miracle baby. She needed to loosen up and see the bright side. Almost doesn't count, et cetera, et cetera.

I was rattling the ice in my fourth drink when Uncle Billy crutched back over. Mirth made his red puffy face look like it wanted to explode.

"You're the funniest son-of-a-bitch I ever met. Know what you are? You're a friggin' card-and-a-half."

"What are you talking about?"

"They're inside opening presents, and I seed what you give the kid. Now how in hell did you think up a thing like that?"

Instantly, I got the sweats. I had forgotten all about my gifts. I had brought a nice gift and a gag gift. Stuck them both in the big pile. The nice gift was a beautiful hardback illustrated edition of *The Complete Mother Goose* and the gag gift came with apologies to Flannery O'Connor. Two Sundays before, this actress I'm seeing—on and off—dragged me to a massive Orange County junk-fest. For six dollars I bought a large hollow bible. Inside I put—what else?—a pack of condoms, a pint of bourbon and a deck of pornographic playing cards. For my infant godson.

"Damn!" I blurted. I left Uncle Billy, splash-filled my glass, and hustled into the house. Since I had almost killed the kid, I had lost all latitude—the space to make jokes in mild bad taste. I would apologize and find the real gift.

When I entered the room, the gaggle of ladies went quiet. They were disgusted with me. I could smell the fumes. This, in itself, was something of a joke. At least five of them had already told me what great fans they were of *Dawn Becomes the Darkness*. Every day they ate fattening lunches and reveled in the sleazy capers of Dawn Desiree, a character I created. By day, she runs an interior decorating business in Beverly Hills. By night she operates an escort service to the stars.

One reason the show is a mega-hit is we use celebrity look-a-likes. We change the names. You'd be surprised how many out-of-work actors are Rob Lowe, John Travolta, Woody Allen, Madonna, or Elvis Presley look-alikes. Sure, we use dead ones, too. They're the best, actually, being less likely to sue. Recently, we'd put in Bogart, Marilyn, and Winston Churchill. The producers have only drawn the line on Abe Lincoln and Martin Luther King. Frequently, I have Dawn give sensible advice to politicians on zoning matters, tax law, and international crises. Last week, though, she told someone resembling George Bush, the younger, that we should have gone all out and bombed Tehran. All the show's regulars have acute or latent psychological disorders. None of them can manage money. Without exception, they want what they can't have. Even when we let them get it, they immediately want something else. Without exception, their desires are lewd and disgraceful and normally involve shocking betrayals of spouses, close friends, relatives, or associates.

I looked past the revolted ladies and found Loni. My smile cracked like a shattered windshield. Her face twisted and wrinkled like crushed silk.

"I'm just glad Mom and Dad aren't alive to see the mess you've made of my baby's big day."

"That was a joke gift, a literary joke. You were an English major. O'Connor used the hollow bible bit in 'Good Country People.' It was meant to be funny."

I looked around the room. Silence. I hated seeking their approval. I recognized Mrs. Fanshaw. Outside the church, she had gushed and asked for my autograph. She referred to *Dawn Becomes the Darkness* as "my story." She said she lived for it. Pathetic. Now, her bunched-up jaw emanated outrage.

Ridiculous. I decided to take charge. I put down my glass.

"I got a nice gift, too," I explained, crossing the crowded room. "I'll find it."

I kicked a couple of purses and stepped on a lady's foot.

I plunged into the pile, flailing at presents, flattening boxes, popping bows, dislocating cards. I couldn't find my package. I couldn't even remember what color wrapping they used.

"David!" Loni yelled. "Cut it out! Go outside! Have another drink!"

I picked up a box with bluebirds circling blue baby carriages. I tugged at the paper.

"The gift I got is nice."

"Go away. You're drunk."

"I'm not." I was only a little drunk.

"I was an idiot to invite you."

"You had to invite me. I'm your only brother. Don't you think you're overdoing the anger bit? You shouldn't be so uptight." I was trying to cut tape with my fingernail. "Lighten up: I got him something that'll take you back. You like to go back."

"Whatever it is, I'll burn it."

It got to me—her reaming me out like that. I got a temper, too.

My voice hiked to a higher pitch. "I can't believe you're so pissed. You should be grateful I saved the little bastard."

"David!"

"Here's my gift." I tore up the bluebirds. "Mom used to read this to us."

I raked through the tissue and yanked out two pairs of blue pajamas.

Peter was next to me. He clamped my elbow.

"Let's go. You need a nap."

I dropped the box, suddenly depressed as hell, the steam all gone, docile and defeated. I picked up my glass. He led me through the crowd. My shoulders slumped. He got behind me going up the stairs and placed his hand on the small of my back.

"Why's she so mad?"

"No one's mad."

"I got him before he hit."

"I know. I got it on tape."

"What's a little water? It was holy water."

"She'll listen later. She's just all worked up. She's been look-ing forward to this day for more than a decade. With what she's gone through, the thought of losing the baby…"

He let the sentence hang. It made sense—having the baby had been her fulfillment. All those pregnancy specialists; her settling her heels into chrome stirrups in Boston, Baltimore, New York, and Philadelphia; him squirting his juice into more and more test tubes. At her age, thirty-nine, it took guts to go in vitro. I slumped even more.

"Tell her nothing really happened. Nothing bad."

"It's your parents, too."

Both of them had died during her pregnancy. It was another miracle she didn't miscarry. Now, I was the only one left—my parents' flawed and suspect surrogate.

He opened the guest room door and gave me a little push. I was going on ice. He tried to take my glass. I tugged it and raised it way up. He'd have to wrestle me for it. He gave me another push, harder this time. I was letting this twerp move me around. It was my penance. I stepped back. He pulled the doorknob.

"Get some sleep!"

Click.

Who could sleep?

I sat on the futon that doubled as my bed. I was a prisoner in Loni's study, her den of genealogical research, a cave of archival exhumation. I looked around. At the large oak desk, she worked with Xeroxed piles of telephone listings from all municipalities in Michigan, Ohio, Illinois, Indiana, New York, Delaware, Pennsylvania, New Jersey, and the New England states. She wrote letters of inquiry to people with our various family names. In a metal file cabinet, she kept reams of old letters, all dutifully catalogued and summarized. What was she going to do with this stuff? I guess the same thing somebody might do with a beer can collection—keep it until he finds somebody who wants to look at it.

Occasionally, on my visits, I wanted to look at it, though I could only take so much. The dead have their weight, a heavy soaked compress. These old letters—hundred-year-old letters—sagged with the mass of defunct personality. There were all those details, desires, and dreams that had nowhere to go. Everybody referred to in them was dead. It didn't bother Loni. Among the dead, she thrived. The living were a different story. I bothered her.

My biggest crime was my refusal, over three marriages, to try for a male heir, a name bearer into oblivion. But if you knew anything about my wives—number one, a booking agent for nightclub comedians; number two, a famous-faced no-name seductress on a popular coffee commercial; number three (the divorce decree now a little more money, Maalox, and mayhem away), an aerobics instructor who had danced in the back row of a Denise Austin workout video—if you knew my wives (and me!), you'd appreciate how we did the human race a favor. They were all non-procreative types, all purely present, ahistorical, connoisseurs of state-of-the-art (non-surgical) birth control procedures, thoroughly schooled in the uses and abuses of that inventory of foams, gels, plugs, patches, and pills. Loni couldn't fathom it; she was a throwback who had gone to the last limit of reproductive technology. To Loni, we lived before ourselves and we should live after—in the smattering of genes, in the resonance of a name, in the intricacies of story.

In her forays into the past, she had investigated our father's branch, tracked it—no, us—from Mansfield, Ohio back to Mansfield, Connecticut in the 1850s and then through Boston, losing the thread—for now—with Francis Higginson's arrival at Massachusetts Bay on the Arbella in 1630, the year of the Puritan Great Migration. Our mother's family posed the more daunting task. Loni's work had only taken her back four generations. She was currently stalled out with our great, great maternal grandfather Thomas Durning, a twelve-year-old immigrant who arrived in New York in 1878. Ten years later, he managed to get a mortgage on a fifty-acre farm in Lancaster, Pennsylvania. No one knew the Irish county he came from. Apparently, he refused to say, staking his life not on the stale old world but the fresh new one. All Loni knew about Thomas's wife, Mary, was her maiden name—Hanratty—and that they met (their daughter—my great grandmother—recalled in a letter to her granddaughter—my mother) in Harrington, Delaware, where Mary taught school. In her busy future, Loni had all these trips to take—Ireland, England, Delaware—and all these pasts to connect through lines of nomenclature and dates, hoping to give the past a connect-the-dots presence, to transfix the amorphous slither-slick of lost time into a legible chart and then into a good story.

In my mildly woozy state, I was unnerved by her littered desk, its poltergeist spew of papers, file folders, index cards. It got me in a cube-rattling parody of escape. I stalked the room and looked out the window. Cars everywhere. I was hoping all the Mrs. Fanshaws would leave, so I could come out. I went back and forth, window to door with time again slowing down, the minutes not moving, my life suspended in a frozen solution.

I stopped pacing and stared ahead. The walls were much more prisoner friendly. They were a museum of restored photographs, images under glass. Many were familiar—my eighteen-year-old mother posing in 1943 with four boys trying to be men, baby faces in Air Force uniforms. I knew the two boys in the middle—I don't know their names, so I won't make them up—were shot down in separate places, one over Italy, the other above the Pacific. The hum of many motors is ruptured by a booming crash and a blizzard of smoke and then death—real death (theirs, others)—comes sometime during more blasts, farther falls, and emphatic crashes. The gravitational pull flurried my stomach and nudged me toward other frames. Eight years later, my mother and father sit side by side in a honeymoon rowboat. Her lacy, black curly hair crushes my father's shoulder. He wears a tie, a blazer, and a tentative smile, as if not quite composed, unready for the Eye, maybe unsettled about sex—they were virgins, I'm sure—and not quite prepared for the pressing weight of happiness: happiness in the form, some twelve months later, of me, my father's heir, and five years after that, of Loni. I found myself in many of the photos, my child-self, but these did not interest me as much as the stranger faces staring from stark, somber fields of gray and white. Most of these relatively unknown people were related to me. That young woman alive in the bubble dress under the bonnet and holding the parasol stands caught like one of Monet's plump aristocrats. She is my father's maternal grandmother, Martha Whitney. But suddenly, years later, ten years before I was born, she is lying in a box, swaddled in satin, hands tangled with rosary beads, dead at seventy-two from an arrested heart achieved in the depths of sleep. Somebody took a picture.

I stepped left and found the three grandfather Thomas Durning photos. In one he is a boy, probably seventeen, wearing puffy black pantaloons and a white open-neck shirt with rolled sleeves. Saddled atop a gray horse, he stares sternly at the Eye, his black hair cropped, his face slashed by a beginner's mustache. His strangely informal slouch is so unlike the wedding photo. His hair now parts down the middle and his mustache covers like a caterpillar brush. He stands starched within the tight shirt and high-buttoned black suit. A three-inch cravat gags him. My great great grandmother floats fluffy in wedding lace. Her round cherub face sinks behind a veil that tumbles from a stitched, beaded cap. One frame to the left, they assemble in a family pose. Seated on two ends of a wooden bench, Thomas and Mary wear rough

JOHN WENKE

but clean clothing; he, a stiff Sunday suit of worsted wool, a white shirt buttoned to his neck, and scuffed boots; she, a homespun calico dress, loosely cut to contain the expansive maternal girth. Thomas has short black hair splashed with gray and a rough rounded face. It's the tough-guy look, like Hemingway in Paris. His rigidly composed face seems barely to harness the etched crinkles cut around his eyes and the dark creases cleaving his forehead. His left arm settles around the shoulders of his eldest son, Thomas, an adolescent boy, somber faced, seemingly bored, my great uncle Tom who will die at Flanders during the First World War. His sister, Mary, two years younger, sits hip close to her brother and wears a white cotton dress with a lace-trimmed collar. Great Aunt Mary's little girl hands are folded, her eyes and mouth fixed in that grim old-photo fright. She will live until 1942, when she will die of pneumonia, the grandmother of our second cousin, Uncle Billy. It's disturbing to see what this beautiful child has come to. On mother Mary's lap sits my great grand-father John, a boy of two dressed in a bag-like white gown that seems linen. These rigid poses owe everything to slow shutter speeds and a quaint reverence for representation. But there is John, the universe's newest scamp, unable to contain himself, the life force let loose, twisting into a hilarious laugh, his little round face a smear of unfocused mirth, a blur on the plate of perfection, the spastic joy of infancy erasing the rigor of slow-baked impressions.

Thomas feels relieved to escape the hot studio. He steps outside into the searing, cloudless day. He sweats with a lilting sense of rectitude. Personally, he doesn't care if his pho-tograph is ever taken, but Mary wants it and Thomas feels proud—warm—that he is spending the money and giving up this whole July day to a twelve-mile wagon ride, the awful lurching and sweating in these gone-to-church clothes, the children excited and wild from the open flatbed ride, tricked into good humor by the promise of ice cream—five portions

62

for twenty-five cents—expensive but worth it. All worth it. The day will remain to be savored.

In a frame, in his later years, he'll be able to look at the beautiful faces of his children's youth. Nothing remains of his own hard days, only the memory of hands blistered from cutting bog on their humpy, wasted plot in the sad lands west of Donegal. One day, in the early morning after his drunken father had beaten him, he left a note and walked away. The worthless rat had again dared to strike his sainted mother and Thomas struck back for her. Even now as Thomas pats the flank of Black and strokes the mane of Blue, as he breathes the roused, always settling street dust and watches the sidewalk throng massing at and passing the entrances to the general store and saloon, as he waits for Mary and the children to return from the wooden outhouse in the alley behind, he still feels the dull dig of guilt for running away, and he still intends to write his mother soon with promises of money and passage to America. He is now getting well ahead of the bank, and with the railroad coming through next spring, he will soon be ahead of the world. Thomas tightens Blue's buckler and moves to the rail, tugging the cord, sad with the thought that he cannot remember his good mother's face, disturbed that now, at the age of thirty-two, he is three years older than the shadowy face and empty features that drift beyond memory and focus only in the vaporous flashing of forgotten dreams. Mary is always right: in old age they will love the faces of their little children.

Thomas hears them before he sees them spill from behind the building. Then hand in hand with little Mary, holding John to his chest, leading his wife and elder son, he marches down the planked, cluttered walk to the general store. He buys five portions of ice cream. They eat at a wooden table and saunter back along the boards. Black and Blue see them and fidget in their traces. Young Thomas scampers into the flatbed and then the father lifts young Mary, takes John from his mother and hands him up. And then for the first time in years, he lifts Mary's full mother-weight, swooping her around in a laughing dance. The children squeal and adults whoop. He slumps to catch his breath. With a surge, he grabs her again and swishes her around, and then with a one-two step he climbs the creaking wagon and settles his wife—his great love—mother-weight and all—into the seat. Holding his back and moaning in a show of mock pain, he leaps to the street, unties the reins and leads Black and Blue around. With the children still kicking and laughing, Thomas climbs up, sits down, and shakes the horses into motion.

Later that day, Thomas stills feels dreamy. He leaves the fierce light and heat to see why Yellow the mule honks and whines in the barn. He bucks in the stall. Thomas unties the cord and swings the gate. Yellow scrapes and bumps the boards. The hooves skitter among shadows. He sees an oozing bruise on her left hind fetlock. To gain a full view, Thomas leads her by the mane and swings open the barn door. He pats her flank and glances into space. The low light of this golden evening streaks through the maple and illumines a trellised, gossamer threadwork. He pats her hind and settles down, searching for the wound, but he never gets low enough to see. With the speed of a trip hammer, Yellow kicks both feet and bucks. The left hoof grazes his hip but the right one pummels him dead center to his belly. His breath departs in one raspy gust. As Yellow limps and snorts to the stall, Thomas lifts, staggers and falls flat-back down. His arms spread wide and then his body curls. In the doorway dirt, he cannot find voice to call. He writhes and kicks, waiting for the pain to pass. The mouth blood mostly seeps until it gushes and seeps again.

Thomas finds his father and raises a howling cry. He and Mother drag him to bed. Thomas saddles Black and rides for the doctor.

In the bedroom, Dr. Bates leans over, pokes the blue-black distended stomach and backs away.

"I'm sorry, but there's nothing I can do." He turns toward the window, embarrassed. "By tomorrow, he'll be dead. Laudanum will make it easy. Otherwise, it'll be the delirium."

The very next day, an hour before dawn, Thomas becomes one with the dust that drifts beneath the moon.

The door clicked. I turned. Loni was there. She was holding Thomas. My glass was empty and my head much clearer. Loni smiled. I looked away, toward the window, embarrassed.

"Can I come in?"

I almost said, *It's your room.*

"Sure. I'm just looking at the pictures on the wall." I rattled my cubes. "I was thinking about Great Great Grandfather Thomas Durning and how that mulekick ruptured his spleen and God knows what else. Today, they'd whisk him off, cut him open, take the damn thing out, sew everything up and charge the insurance company forty thousand bucks. It's awful it had to happen on the day they took the photo. In that letter I read, Mary said how she was worried the picture wouldn't turn out. It's why she had one taken of him dead. I suppose it hasn't turned up."

"Not yet." She stepped closer, all the way inside the room, and then walked over. "Here, I want you to hold Thomas."

I almost said, *Okay, but you better get a tub of water.* "Sure. I'd be happy to. Love to."

I took him, a kicking bundle. There was a dab of puke stuck to his chin. He wore a New York Mets one-piece outfit.

"Hey! You have him dressed like a loser."

Loni smiled. "Dad loved the Mets, even when they were losers."

Thomas seemed to be gazing into space. He had that baby-face blankness. I held him and went "boo-boo" and made a lot of other silly sounds. I didn't look at Loni, but I knew she was watching me, the anger gone, slipped somewhere far away, my sins forgiven and not to be discussed, my joke gift nullified but not to be forgotten. I didn't look up, just made noises into the blankness. It seemed like everyone was here and they were all laughing at me. Mom and Dad, even the assembled generations. Time collapsed. The room seemed fuller than a photo of the unforgotten dead, stuffed with silence, the moment's latent story, and all those feelings there aren't any pictures for.

Z-Man and the Christmas Tree

My broom stabbed beneath the bottom shelf and slammed the right corner. When I jerked the handle, out tumbled two silver gum wrappers, a skittering mess of pinto beans, some brown lettuce fringed with black rot, a matted dust ball, two quarters, one nickel, and three pennies. There was a crisp cricket corpse, its burnt-matchstick body crumbled into pieces.

I gathered fifty-eight cents and jiggled it to the register. "Here's to the profit margin."

Laura Brown looked up from her spreadsheet. Her green eyes blinked behind gold granny glasses. Straggly gray hair leaked from a purple and white tie-dyed do-rag.

"What's that?"

"Loose change." I held it out. "From under the shelves."

Her thin smile stretched her angular face. "Thanks."

She tossed the coins into the collection jar on the counter. Nina Aspen, a twelve-year-old cheerleader over on High Street, was in need of a bone marrow transplant. Laura looked at the clock. It was almost one. "I thought you'd be gone by now."

"I wanted to finish. Do you know where the dustpan got to?"

She shrugged and slid inside her spreadsheet. I looked up and down the shelves. They were lined with paper bags filled with dry goods, a healthy-for-life load heavy on whole grain breads, lentils, green pasta, brown rice, unbleached organic flour, dried beans, dried fruit, barley, yeast, nuts, and spices.

"Did you take care of the McFarland issue?"

Laura was now flipping through a stack of cards. Mike McFarland, a local plumber, had phoned in his order yesterday, a strictly forbidden thing. At the Willimantic Food Cooperative, you dropped your card off by Monday for

Thursday pick-up. Laura usually stood firm, but McFarland was a charter member who did all her plumbing—labor free, parts at cost. Even a squeaky-clean idealist like Laura had to do special favors.

"No sweat. He can pick up his stuff with everybody else."

Tonight, between 4:00 and 8:00 p.m., members would claim their groceries. After finding their alphabetized bags, they'd work their way along the coolers for specialty juices, eggs, and yogurt and then to the freezer for weighed portions of whatever fish Laura had gotten flash-frozen from her old commune pal Spanky Daniel. He ran a big wholesale outfit up in Boston. Beyond the sliding freezers were self-serve taps for honey, real maple syrup, and olive oil. My eyes stopped at produce. The dustpan was stuck between an open fifty-pound sack of potatoes and a mound of acorn squash.

The bell jangled. The door whisked open. My wife, Lucy, was carrying a box the size of a bookshelf speaker.

"Hey!" I shouted. I quickly swept up the dirt.

"I only got a few minutes. I want to show you what I came up with."

I dumped the dirt and hurried to the front. Lucy had set the box on the counter and was unzipping her purple L.L. Bean down jacket. She plucked the white ball atop her red ski cap. A brownish, bottle-dyed pile of ringlets tumbled to her shoulders. Laura was pulling open the flaps. Behind them the display window was cluttered with twinkling Christmas lights, gnarled bunches of holly, silver bells, and evergreen branches. Between the miniature Hanukkah bush and potted Christmas tree was an electric menorah and one of those multi-colored Kwanzaa candle holders. On a bed of hay lay a manger scene—three goats, two cows, and one horse hunched around the swaddled infant. On the snowy roof of the Palestinian stable was Santa, his sleigh, and reindeer. A few elves were mixed with the shepherds and some brightly colored boxes were piled at the foot of the manger.

"Whew!" Lucy said, rubbing her hands together. "The chill goes right through you."

Laura was hauling a Styrofoam mold out of the box. She pulled the pieces apart.

"Oh, Lucy! This is beautiful. Daddy'll love it!"

Laura was holding a cuckoo clock, its little cigar-like weights dangling at the ends of golden chains.

"Hey! You found one."

"Finally," Lucy said. "It's all wood. Two hundred bucks. Margaret Defoe told me about this little store out in Andover. I got someone to cover my study hall, and I'm skipping lunch. I need to run though. I'm giving a test seventh period."

"I'll get it in the mail," I said.

"Can you, Tom? I know you're tired, but I'm in a bind. I won't be home till after seven. I promised Jane Elkins I'd stay with her mother while she shopped."

Mrs. Elkins was end-stage breast, bone, and brain cancer.

"I'm not that tired. I'll get it done. No sweat."

Everyday I'm up at four and drive a two hundred and twelve copy paper route for *The Chronicle*. I stuff half the copies into blue tubes and fling the other half on to lawns, porches, and doorsteps. This job started out as a kind of self-help manipulation. If I have to get up early, I won't drink much the night before. I'm not an alcoholic, but I can be a problem drinker. I like the taste of booze, the swish in my mouth, the rush. I could probably dump the paper route and hold myself together, but I find I like the life—the early morning darkness, the quiet. It's a little like driving a squad car on pre-dawn patrol, though nobody wants to shoot me or call me "white pig," and I don't want to shoot, boink, club, or lock up anyone. I get home by seven, wake Lucy up, make breakfast, and push her out the door. She teaches algebra and geometry at South Mansfield High. I do the dishes, straighten up, shower, and get to the co-op by nine.

I don't really need the job. Lucy is the breadwinner. I retired at forty-eight after twenty-five years on the Hartford force. But I like the work. I push a broom, fill bags, make phone calls, stock shelves, rock salt the pavement. On Fridays I deliver orders to shut-ins, and I always stick around to talk. My head never feels like it wants to explode, and it doesn't even bug me that my hippie-dippy sister-in-law is my boss.

"Do you think it'll break?" Lucy asked.

"I'll put the box in another box and pack it around with balled-up newspapers. Your old man can kill some time reading the wrapping." Their father lives in Naples, Florida, and Lucy and I live in his old house. Like me, Lucy is a retread, a little worn down. Her ex gambled their house away, so the divorce sent her back at age thirty-five to live with her father. There weren't any kids. After Lucy and I married late last year, the old man turned himself into a snowbird. When he comes north for the summer, he stays half the time with us, the other half with Laura, her husband, and their two teenage boys. The mother's been dead five years.

"Besides, I still have to mail our package to Charlie. I'll do them together." Charlie's my only kid from a marriage that ended nine years ago. To get away from me, his mother had moved to Pittsburgh. He's twenty-three now. It's awful to think about, but he's a rookie cop. He says he's providing an important service. But in a few years his head will hurt like jackhammers, and his neck muscles will burn like they're on fire.

"Dad'll probably get it late."

"I'll pay extra. They'll get it there. It's only the twenty-second."

"Well, I hope so. Love you! I got to run."

I helped Lucy bundle into her coat and I walked her to the door. She pointed up the street.

"Hah! Look who's coming! Just what every day needs."

"Oh, no!" Laura moaned. She was bending her head to see around the menorah. "Z-Man's limping worse than usual."

Lucy pecked my lips and pulled her hat over her eyebrows. "He'll want something. He always does. Before I went shopping, I stopped home to get some pads and I heard them—Marge yelling about the beer being all gone. There was this big crash, and then she really started screaming. Just don't let him tie up your day."

"No problem," I said.

"Maybe he's not even coming here," Laura mumbled, squinting up the street.

"I'm gone," Lucy called.

The door jangled, the wind whooshed, and Lucy jogged to our good car, a new maroon Taurus. I drive my old bomb, a 1999 Dodge Durango. It used to be black; but now it's like me—getting gray with streaks of white and a few specks of rust. She zoomed up Main Street into the screaming sunlight. Z-Man raised a hand to wave to her, but she was out of sight in seconds. He was bundled to the chin with a long black wool coat. A red muffler wrapped his neck and bulged like the layers of a coiled anaconda. His hair looked like greasy black lines drawn by a three-year-old. It was parted crooked down the middle with running strands plastered on both sides of his balding skull. The cold gusty wind had burned his face red. The furrows flanking his nose seemed leftovers from a slashing. But the lines were not scars. They were simply the way his face was caving in. And he *was* limping.

He crossed the street and seemed on the verge of falling. With arms swaying and hips swinging, he plopped his right foot before him and dragged his left foot behind. His mouth twisted and his eyes blinked. When he saw us staring from behind sprayed ice crystals and waffle snowflakes, he made his mouth into an oval and let his upper dentures drop like a guillotine.

"He's *gr-oss!*" Laura sneered. "Why's he act like that?"

"He thinks it's funny. Wait'll you see him do it with a mouthful of corn chips."

"I hope he doesn't come in here."

"With a limp like that he's looking for me."

"You do too much for him. It's why he won't grow up."

"I feel for the guy. He's not all there."

In the last days of Vietnam, Z-Man had gotten shot in the head. Now he was doing life on disability.

"You forget I'm a local. I knew him before he went to that war. He never was right. He's always been a problem."

The doorbell clanged. Hinges screeched. The wind swished. Z-Man dragged through the door and pounded his naked hands. "Colder than a bitch's witch!"

Laura was starchy most of the time—it comes with being pure in a grimy world—but when she got mad her lips puckered. "Shut the door! Heating oil's more than three dollars a gallon."

Z-Man looked at me. "Hey, Tom, tell me how to get in without opening the frigging door."

"She just wants you to *close* the door."

I reached behind him and pushed it shut.

"Yeah!" she huffed. "And act civilized!"

"I ain't staying but for a minute. Hey! It's hot in here."

He grabbed the end of his frayed muffler, lifted it over his head, and unraveled it. Around his neck was a hard, white orthopedic collar, one he had first worn last Halloween. Lucy and I had been sitting on the porch, waiting for the kids to trick-or-treat. It was still dusk when Marge and Z-Man came tumbling out of their rundown saltbox next door. She was screaming about blood money and being sick of him not flushing the toilet. He called her "Big Gal" and slapped her behind, yelling "Get along, little doggie!" She was waving her arms real spastic, like she was fighting her way through cobwebs. He tripped and sprawled face down into her hips. She got him in a choke hold, her right arm clamping his face, and then she pulled him around the sidewalk like he was a two-legged steer. With her free fist, she punched his face again and again.

"I thought you took that collar back to the hospital. They did you a favor letting you borrow it."

"Well, Tom, I figured I might just need it again. You never know. I got a little woman whose middle name is whiplash."

"You should've returned it," Laura snarled. "It's more deadbeat stuff. And you wonder why I shut down your account."

"Tell your boss mamma I had a relapse."

"You need to cut it out," I said. "This loud stuff turns people off."

Z-Man lowered his head. "Me sorry. Me a loser."

Laura huffed and rubbed her hands. "I got things to do in the back. If you leave, lock up." She stomped away.

"I'm wondering," he whispered, "if you can give me a hand."

Laura was right. I did too much for him, but I always felt like, what the hell, the guy's a mess, unemployable, and a basic casualty. He locks his keys in the house or drops one down a drain or needs a chair glued together. Or with his arm suddenly in a sling he needs help carrying groceries or maybe the faucet is squirting and the toilet won't flush. He never asks for money, though once he needed a lift to Cash Advance just as Lucy and I were heading north to see an arty movie in Storrs. We wound up being late. Lucy won't go into a movie late. For punishment, she made me drive to East Hartford for some dubbed Japanese junk. We argued all the way and got to bed late—all because I had to help Z-Man pre-spend his disability check so he and Marge could punch one another out on pizza and beer.

"I'm pretty beat today."

"I need to haul a Christmas tree. I got it picked out."

"I got things to do, but I'll drive you over tonight, after I get off. Tell them to have it wrapped and ready."

"I didn't mean *buy* it, man. I mean, I picked it out. It's still in the ground."

"What?"

"In the state park. Out behind our yards."

"I'm not going to steal a Christmas tree."

"It ain't stealing. The park belongs to the people. Besides, there are thousands of trees out there. This is just a little one. Marge gave me the word. She wants a live tree in the living room, and she wants it there by five. If I don't make the place look like Christmas, I'm dog meat. She'll frigging kick me out."

"It's your house. She can't kick you out."

"She can. She will. I just need a little help. My knee's gone out again, and my neck is bone-fused or something. It'll take half an hour. Tops. We can use your wheelbarrow to haul it. I'll move the branches so we can make it up the path."

"I was up at four today and you want me to dig up a tree?"

"It's a runt. I can almost dig it out with my bare hands."

"I got to get two packages in the mail."

"It won't take long. Twenty minutes. Tops."

I brushed my hands together, went around the counter, and locked the cash register.

"If it turns into a big job, I'm done. Marge'll just have to kick you out."

Everywhere I looked the Christmas season jingled. Fake strands of icicles hung from the antiqued facade of Zeising Brothers Book Emporium. The streetlamps swirled with plastic holly. Clusters of artificial poinsettias were stuck on top of light casings. Across Main Street, the Romantic Willimantic banner was rimmed with red, green, and yellow lights. Z-Man and I walked down Main Street, our feet crunching rock salt and gravel. We passed the little shed where children lined up nightly to visit Mr. and Mrs. Claus. From Discount Tapes and CDs, Bing Crosby crooned the words to "Silver Bells."

As Z-Man limped, he gripped my elbow, maybe to keep himself from falling, maybe to keep me from running away. He'd been going on about the sex scandal rocking South

Mansfield High. "He had this hidden camera rigged inside a locker to tape the boys in the shower."

On Tuesday, Lucy and I had watched a news report on the Hartford station showing gym teacher Jake Jermin being led to a police car. The cops confiscated a computer and two boxes of CDs. Four of the boys were now claiming he had abused them. Jake used to be one of the people Lucy liked and now he was in the County Detention Center.

"He drilled this peephole and twisted it so it looked like normal vandalism stuff. You'd think he would've seen enough buck naked guys over the years, but noooo, he had to take some pictures home. What do you think'll happen to the guy?" Z-Man asked.

"Hard time. He'll do five to ten, maybe more if he put any of it out on the net. The judges don't like child porn, and they don't like molesters. You can be sure of one thing. Your prison population won't be too nice to Jake Jermin. And it'll serve him right."

Every now and then, in the year before I quit the force, I'd boink the heads of certain perpetrators. Sex offenders, wife beaters, killers, pushers. Your basic scumbags. I'd have them cuffed from behind, and as I lowered their heads to slip them into the car, I'd shove them a little too quickly and boink their heads on the door frame. There'd be this thud, like somebody dropped a stuffed leather bag. It made my day. Jake Jermin was just the kind of creep whose head I would've boinked.

"You're too tough," Z-Man grunted. "We live in For-give-a-Mistake Land. O.J.'s proof of that. Jake was feeding a hunger. He probably has a mental disability."

"He has three daughters and a wife, and they're done for. All because he's a pervert."

"Hey, Tom!" In the middle of the street, facing the other way, a squad car had stopped. Fred Parini had his face out the window. "You got a minute."

"Sure."

"Let me turn around."

As I stopped to wait, Z-Man pushed away. "He's got zip on me, the frigging mental case." He pushed ahead, his limp rapidly improving.

Having come around, Fred leaned across the passenger seat.

From up the street Z-Man yelled, "Hurry up, man! Only three shopping days left till bankruptcy."

"What's his problem?" Fred said.

"He's upset that you've arrested him a few times."

"I do him a favor when I arrest him. Get him loose from that crazy lady. A few more beers and she'll kill him right up." Over the radio came a report of a wreck out on Route 32. "I got to run. What I wanted to know is whether you got any extra flounder. I just heard from Janine that her folks are coming for dinner. We ordered a pound. I could use another pound."

"I'll take care of it."

"By the way, what's he got you doing now?"

"He has me digging up a Christmas tree."

"Hah! You oughta mail that bozo to Borneo."

"Hey, it's Christmas."

The cruiser peeled away, lights flashing, and I scuffled along the crunchy pavement. Z-Man had passed the great stone walls of the bank and was dragging his leg across a rutted, graveled parking lot, heading for the foot bridge, an erector-set contraption that rose beam by beam between bare oak and maple limbs and extended sixty feet above the Willimantic River. He was now hauling himself up the first stretch of metal steps. By the time I caught up, he was on the first landing, dragging his foot across the pimpled metal grill. The river eased along at low water. A few rocks humped in the drift like the scratched gray backs of sculpted sea lions.

"That limp doesn't slow you down."

"Necessity is the frigging mother of prevention. Fuzz sees me and all of a sudden it's time to pork Eric Ziemon."

The metal walkway rattled and the wind whipped our ears.

Upstream, two boys were floating in a canoe, poking holes in thin ice sheets that lined the shore.

"Fred said he was coming after you for suspicion."

"What!" he screamed. "I ain't done nothin'! Ask Marge, but Marge ain't around. She's out to Coventry seeing her sister."

"Relax. I'm kidding. Fred just wanted some fish."

We were clumping down the steps on the far side, just above a sheer ninety-foot drop where last summer a young girl had fallen and cracked her skull. The paramedics found her face down in the water. She never woke up. We got on the ramp that runs out to Pleasant Street. Our houses were right across from the foot bridge, the only two on the block. Z-Man was paying a subsidized mortgage on his saltbox. Its white paint flaked like fungus petals. Three roof shingles flapped in the wind. The rain gutter tilted from the eave. Lucy and I lived in the brick rancher next door. Our windows were edged with lights. Two spotlights and a color wheel sat in the middle of our lawn.

"I'm going to put the cuckoo clock inside. Meet me out back in five minutes."

I expected Z-Man to be standing where the property line gives way to the state park's border and its packed trees. But he wasn't there. I left the wheelbarrow, spade, blue cotton drop cloth, and rope near the path and trudged to his brown back door. A cluttered hall opened into the kitchen.

"Hey, Z-Man! Let's move it."

His muffled voice descended.

"I'm upstairs. I got the runs. It's another reason I can't do no digging. I bend over, and it'd be like an open faucet."

His house had a constant mildew smell, the sort of musky swamp rot you get from a wet towel left to stew for weeks in the trunk of a car. The place had a warehouse feel—cluttered and dirty. Every room had half-emptied boxes, the flaps up. Towels and spoons were scattered on the floor. A pile of ratty sweaters was waiting to be tripped over. In the corner of the kitchen, the trash can overflowed with empty milk jugs, crushed pizza boxes, a clump of wet paper towels, and four open cartons of Chinese food—the insides coated with brown and yellow slime. To the left was a slumping pile of beer cans, maybe two hundred of them, each piece worth a nickel deposit. The pile gave off that stale stench of loser taprooms at two in the morning. I hated the smell of the place, but Lucy hated seeing it even more. A few weeks ago, she and I had stopped to get signatures for a school funding referendum and found Z-Man cooking at a boiling pot, using a fork to fling spaghetti on the wall. The strands hit and fell behind a counter. When one finally stuck, he turned off the coil and said dinner was ready. What I had taken for yellowed stucco turned out to be a crusted web-work of dried pasta.

The stairway creaked and footsteps thumped.

"We got to move it," I called. Scattered on the living room floor were pieces of a smashed lamp. Z-Man limped down the steps, tugging his belt two notches too tight.

"After we get the tree, I'll make the house squeaky clean. Let Marge come back to a little Christmas spirit."

On the forest path, Z-Man limped ahead, while I pushed the clattering wheelbarrow. The rippled earth jostled the wheel and sent it skittering through ruts covered by the crunchy swish of brown leaves. The bouncing wheel sent tingles into my elbows. All around me the trunks of trees were like bare poles with dangling arms and twisted fingers. I could easily imagine the trees waking up, stepping out of the earth, and turning into a marching army of crazed skeletal monsters. First, they'd crush and scatter Z-Man. Then they'd rip me from the earth and fling me into space.

Where a stand of evergreens darkened the day, I pointed to a round three-footer.

"How about that one?" I said. Z-Man stopped, and I set the wheelbarrow down. "I have a big plastic pot in the garage. It'll fit perfect. I can set it up in your living room. I'll even plant it for you in the spring."

"That's too small. I got one picked out already. Up here."

The tree he wanted was six feet tall and full bellied.

"It's too big."

"It's perfect. Marge has decorations from some of her marriages."

Marge was forty-something and had three bad marriages to show for it. She was also mother to two grown girls, loose in the world, probably hanging on somewhere near the end of the road.

"I'll dig no more than fifteen minutes. If I don't get around the root-ball by then, I'm taking one of those three-foot jobs. If Marge doesn't like it, she can eat my shorts."

Z-Man bent over and whooped, cranking his torso back up in one strained motion, his face a gasping spasm of laughter. "I'd pay to see that! Soak 'em in beer and she'd eat 'em right off your butt."

He whooped some more. It was getting on my nerves, so I shook my head and fell to work. After raking the leaves and exposing the ground, I was surprised at how easily the loamy soil found its way into mounds of tumbling stone and flint-like shale that might have been arrowheads. It didn't take long, and I grabbed the trunk and wobbled the tree. I got down into a three by four ditch, shoved the spade clear under the roots, and lifted the tree straight up. With the roots concentrated in a mass and most of the dirt knocked off, I slow-danced the sucker right into the wheelbarrow. I looked for Z-Man, who was five feet behind me, kicking a mess of leaves into a pile.

"Hey, Z, you're gonna have to walk alongside and hold the top of the tree. Otherwise, I won't be able to work the han—" I stopped, shocked by what I saw, a white human hand visible through the leaves.

"God help us! So that's it!"

"What's it?" he squealed. He pointed to the sky and screamed, "Look at that bird! It's a frigging white heron."

I was out of the ditch. I brushed away the leaves. In seconds, Marge's stone-set face, eyes clamped shut, seemed a twisted mask. Brown crumpled leaves stuck to her frizzled gray hair.

"You killed her and wanted me to bury her."

"That's not it!" His hands were clawing his hard white collar like it was choking him. He was looking into the trees. "You're just digging a hole. You're digging up a Christmas tree."

"I'm taking you into custody."

"You ain't a cop."

"Sure I am. All I did was turn in my badge."

"Look, Tom, I can't be doing time. I'd be prison-bitched from here to the moon."

"Are you even sure she's dead? You can't always be sure they're dead."

He didn't answer. I walked over and knelt down. I put the back of my right fingers to her cheek. It was ivory cold. Marble. I stood up.

"Tom, listen to me. I didn't do it."

"They all say that."

"I didn't, but if *you* don't believe me, the Smokey Bear cats sure as hell won't. I'm trying to *save my ass!* She was drunked up this morning and started doing me with a baseball bat. I was jumping around like some kind of monkey. She chased me to the kitchen and slipped on this beer slick and smashed the back of her head on the handle of the refrigerator. Right on the point of it. Then she didn't move. I pumped her chest and blew in her mouth, but she stayed there. I couldn't find no pulse. I figured the cops'd say I did it, so I piggy-backed her out here. I'd have dug a hole myself but carrying her did something to my neck. I can't even bend over."

"You should've called 911."

"She was gone, and nobody would believe I didn't whomp her behind her head."

Z-Man was making his way around me, the limp all gone, and backing toward the path. I moved toward him, hoping I wouldn't have to run him down and tackle him.

"When the police get the facts, they won't even charge you. Do it this way and you're acting like a guilty man."

"Wooooooo!" he shouted. He held both hands to his cheeks, turned, and bolted down the path.

Behind me leaves were swashing. I looked to find Marge sitting up, her head wobbling. Her eyes were little open slits and her mouth was sagging like a crooked oval.

"Tell that bum—come back—here! Who are you?"

"It's me. Tom Clark. From next door. You know me."

I walked over, knelt on one knee, hooked my hand under her arms and pulled. She was a stack of stones, tumbling and inert. She lay back on the leaves, both hands on her head.

"What happened, Marge? What happened at the house?"

"What—am I doing here? My head—hurts. He drank—all my beer. I—blacked out. Where—am I?"

"He says you hit your head on the refrigerator."

"What we—doing here?"

"Do you remember?"

"That our new tree? Where is—the bum?"

"Yeah, that's your tree. I dug it up. Did he hit you?"

"I'm gonna—beat the stuffing out—of that—no good bum. He drank all my—beer."

"I need to get you to an ambulance."

"We're—in the woods. Did I—black out?"

Maybe Marge fell. Maybe her head needed bashing. These domestic disturbances were never anything but hell. When I was a cop, I often thought that a lot of the citizens I was sworn to protect were more trouble than the career criminals who preyed on them.

"You did. You passed out when I was digging up the tree. You had too much beer."

By the time I talked to the paramedics, I'd have Marge's

story all patched up. I'd have to tell Z-Man what happened.

"Lucky I brought the wheelbarrow, Marge. I'll take you back in it. I'll go to my house and call you an ambulance. Maybe Eric ran ahead to call one himself."

"I'll kill—that bum. He needs to get—the tree up."

I rolled the wheelbarrow over, got behind her, and lifted. I buckled under her weight, but I managed to tilt her on her heels, spin her to the side, and get her big behind into the bed of the wheelbarrow.

"I'm taking you for a little ride."

"I need—a beer. Hair of—the dog. But we ain't got no dog."

"You're going to the emergency room. I think you got a concussion. Maybe a fractured skull."

"What's that?"

She pointed to the wobbled tree.

"Your tree. While I was digging it up, you fell backwards and smashed your head on a pointed rock. You were too drunk to stand."

"Oh. Is it—Christmas yet? I love—Christmas. The Savior—coming."

"In three days."

"I told him—last week. Get—a tree. Silver bells. Put an angel—on top!"

"I'll come back later, after work. I'll get the tree and set it up. Lucy and I will help Eric decorate it. But now we gotta get going. You need to see a doctor and I have to get to the post office." I was pushing my load up the forest path. The back of her head was a bloody mash of leaves and gray hair. "You'll probably be in the hospital for a little while, but with some luck, he'll bring you home for Christmas."

A Good Samaritan Will Stop

Mavis Martin slips the cordless to her left ear. "Got to go. He's here."

His shiny gold Toyota Avalon stops in the middle of the curved street. He sticks his hand out the window and uses his whole arm to fan the air forward.

"Three times he's come to pick me up, and three times he's driven past the driveway. I mean, is that a sign of something?"

A FedEx truck creeps around the Avalon followed by a farting motorcycle.

"I think you're on edge," her sister Eleanor says, "because you never clarified the plans. You should've just told him up-front you only reserved one room."

"It's not just a room. It's a suite. Three hundred a night. Convention rates and it isn't even the season. Not that money matters."

"Worst case scenario: you get the award. He's there to see it. He's standing next to you, this trophy TV guy. Then you get back to the room, and he winds up sleeping on the couch."

Out the window, the Avalon backs down the street but stops as a school bus grunts, screeches, and lumbers past. With the way clear, the car lurches across the road and humps into the driveway, barely missing the tall blooming lilac. In the breeze, the violet cones jostle like pompoms.

"The whole thing could be embarrassing. I mean, what if he thinks I'm forward?"

"You're thinking like a nun. You've been married. He's been married. Just be straight. Pretend you're in a movie. You got the condoms, and he has a choice."

Charles stops his car on the far side of the blacktop. The bright April sun dabs the hood, washes the windshield, and skitters off the roof. The trunk lid pops. After closing the living room curtain, Mavis retreats up the creaking hardwood steps. She plops on her bed and sinks into a mound of pillows. On the ceiling, little lines of light quiver, intersect, and separate.

"He's only ever pecked me on the lips and that was only when he was leaving. He'll take my hand but only if we're crossing a street. How do I read this? I knew how to read Allen. If he had five beers, he wanted sex. Six beers, he fell asleep. But it's different, too, because Charles isn't divorced. *His* wife's dead."

Eleanor isn't listening. She's screaming at her ten and twelve-year-old sons for wrestling in the living room, their turbines spinning out of control after three days of snowbound incarceration. With Dover, Delaware pulsing to the teasing niceties of spring, Mavis is trying to picture the frayed, blasted tundra of suburban Duluth.

Eleanor's breath stabs Mavis' ear. "They cracked one of the coffee table legs right in half."

Waiting for the doorbell to ring, Mavis squeezes her eyes shut. Backyard fir trees bend and swish among whirling gusts and rippling snowdrifts.

"They were rolling around like monkeys. Laughing and jabbering. I smacked both of them. I don't give an *F* how big they are. Why couldn't I have had girls?"

Through the open upstairs window, Mavis hears the car door slam. Leaping up and hustling to the window, she sees Charles sauntering to his open trunk in shiny white slacks and crisp blue Oxford shirt. Under his arm, he carries a matching white jacket. He lifts out a suitcase and a garment bag.

"I had girls," Mavis says, a picture flashing of Marci and Toni sunning on the University of South Carolina campus. "Girls aren't any better. If you can hear the boys, you at least have some idea what they're doing. When my girls were growing up, they were sneaky. They're still sneaky. We were sneaky."

Charles leaves his bags in the driveway and walks up the winding flagstone path. He's early fifty-something, but even with the graying brownish hair, he carries the trim look of Robert Redford youthfulness. At forty-two, Mavis has been dyeing her hair for five years but otherwise keeping it together, only slightly losing out to the slumps of gravity: falling arches, sagging breasts, settling jowls.

Charles climbs the front porch steps. Mavis pulls away from the window.

"He's about to ring the bell. I'll let you know what happens. I'm just nervous as hell."

"Lighten up. He wouldn't be there if he didn't want to be. A power player in his position can get it any time he wants."

The doorbell burbles.

"It's not about sex. I'm worried that he doesn't find me attractive, that he sees me as a one of those awful *companions*. I've only asked him places. He's never asked me anywhere."

The bell rings again.

"Eleanor, let me go. I'll call you Sunday."

After poking the kill switch, Mavis creaks down the steps and drops the phone on the foyer settee. The chimes burble a third time, giving the kind of perky sound you might hear at the beginning of a funny movie about everyday life in heaven.

In the glass, Charles sees his bleached-out ghostly face. Perhaps she's bustling upstairs or in the back locking up or maybe just making him wait like Meg used to do—a balance of power thing. He glances away from the door and eyes his escape route, the curving flagstone walk crowded by pink and white azaleas.

Locks clatter and the door swings wide. Mavis pushes open the glass storm door, smiling. "Sorry for the hold up. I was on the phone with my sister. They're having a blizzard, and her kids are going crazy."

"She's in Minnesota, right? The one with two boys."

"That's Eleanor, freezing on the edge of beautiful Lake Hypothermia."

Charles crosses into the foyer and pats Mavis on the upper left arm. He's very happy to see her. He also wishes he hadn't come. He's looking forward to this weekend away, even as he longs to be hunched at his desk, preparing to launch his trustworthy face into homes, bars, limousines, and conversion vans, taking his viewers on a packaged tour of the day's doings, a cavalcade of sound bites, feel-good fluff, and odd tragedies from near and far—like the baby boy from Franklin, Delaware who yesterday sank through the earth and drowned in a decayed septic tank or last week's shark attack in Pensacola, Florida. The shark bit off a boy's arm, and his uncle wrestled the monster to the beach. A few bullets to the head and they got the arm back. But in two hours and ten minutes Sally Feeney, the weekend anchor, will sign on and announce, "Charles Conroy has the night off." Then Sally will get to tell about the latest mujahideen attack in Kabul—a U. S. soldier shot in the head while waiting in line to buy a soft drink. These stories are always the same: everything is calm until everything explodes.

"I have to feed the cat, check the doors, grab my bags, and we're off."

"Can I help you with anything?"

"No, I'm fine. I'll only be a minute."

She disappears through a set of bi-fold doors.

Meg's voice tickles inside his ears. *This foyer is super gauche. Green marble tile. Velvet couch. Fake stucco walls. All those knickknacks. You put this kind of junk in the house, it means you're trying to prove something. There's a good reason we always went austere.*

I wouldn't worry about it, Meg. I couldn't live here. Cats make me itch. Her living room's like a fancy funeral parlor. A lot of dark wood and leather furniture.

But what would she do to our house?

I don't think it'll get that far.

Then what are you even doing here?

It's a getaway weekend. It's Rehoboth Beach and cocktail parties. She's getting an award. I'll applaud on cue. Beyond that, I don't know. I'm allowed to look. She's a good person. You've been gone three years.

I'm never gone.

From the kitchen, Charles hears the rattle of a cat food bag, a chorus of meows—three cats!—and the pinging rush of pebbly pellets filling large plastic bowls.

"Mavis! I just remembered. I'm supposed to remind you to leave the downstairs toilet seat up."

"Thanks. Poopie sometimes turns over the water."

Already his nose is getting stuffy.

The door is open. Just walk out.

I can't. I just got here.

Something light—a feather—seems to graze his ear. He grabs for it and looks into his open palm. There's nothing there.

Mavis bursts through the doors and clicks into the foyer, dragging a large suitcase on wheels. She lets a garment bag slip to the floor and dumps a leather briefcase on the settee.

"I wanted to make a quick start, but here I am, running late."

"There's no rush. Even if we take our time, we'll be in Rehoboth before five."

You can be home in fifteen minutes.

Meg! Shhh.

"Good," Mavis says. "We can relax a little bit. Cocktails are at six and dinner's at seven. The speeches and stuff come later. I think I'm overdressed for the ride."

Mavis fingers the collar of her black linen jacket.

She'd be better off wearing light slacks and a dark shirt instead of this black pants suit and mauve shirt. She's been a doughty schoolmarm so long that when it's finally time to dress she doesn't know how.

"You're not overdressed at all. You look fine, stylish, in fact."

"Well, I'm nervous is what is it. What if I make a fool out of myself?"

She reaches for the garment bag, but Charles beats her to it. He tucks her briefcase under his arm.

"You can pull the suitcase." He hates wheeled luggage. "And stop worrying. You won't make a fool of yourself."

Fool. Fool. Fool. Fool. Fool.

Stop it, Meg. You'll make me laugh.

"All those people looking at me. What do I know about making a speech?"

"If you're nervous about it, I can drive."

"You can't drive. You said you'd read my speech and let me know how it is."

Fishing for compliments. Pathetic.

"Relax. I'm sure your speech'll be great. If you want, I can read while we drive. No problem. Two eyes, two hands, two feet. I'm always doing two things at once."

As Charles flips page after page of her triple-spaced script, Mavis tries to keep her white-knuckled grip from splitting the wheel into pieces. The traffic cluster of Dover's capitol district has twisted her stomach into knots. She can't wait to get beyond the last few strip malls of south Dover, a seemingly endless spew of dry cleaners, body shops, dollar stores, fast food joints, and pizza parlors. She runs a yellow light and gets to the cyclone fence enclosing Dover Air Force base. Two hundred yards away, a cargo plane with a belly the size of a football field creeps along a runway. Mavis's chest tightens. She imagines a terrorist's bomb transforming the C-130 into a radiating fireball that hurdles their way and turns the blacktop, the fence, her Chevy Tahoe, WXDR's popular newscaster, the state of Delaware's Principal of the Year, her speech, and the whole weekend into a billowing cloud of noxious black smoke.

"That's interesting," Charles mutters.

"What?" Mavis chirps. If the steering wheel were alive, it would be yelping.

"Oh, sorry. I was thinking out loud. I do that sometimes."

"Are you finished? What do you think?"

He rustles the pages. "I have a page and a half to go. Let me finish and we'll talk."

Mavis feels rebuked. She's sure he finds her speech laughable. She finds it laughable. What does she know about the "social good" or "youth's empowerment of the future"? Mavis wants to rip the speech from his hands and stuff it under the seat. Instead, she skirts to the left and passes a wheezing dump truck. But there is no open space. A single row of vehicles heaves forward and slows down.

"Well, I'm done," Charles declares, smiling. He taps the pages on his knees, evens their edges and slides the script into a new beige folder. Outside a rusting white mobile home seems to wobble in front of a squat graying chicken house. A rooster flaps its wings atop a dirt mound. A large black and white cat sleeps in the shade of a willow tree. Only two miles ahead waits the interchange for the Route 1 toll road that will express them to the beach.

"What do you think? I still have time to revise it." Or throw the damn thing out the window.

"Not everybody will know how to take it," Charles says, smiling, "and that's because it's probably too interesting."

Mavis' knuckles stretch her skin.

"Well, I'm not surprised. I knew it was bad. If I'm going to make a fool of myself, let me know. I mean, really. I want the truth. No soft soap."

"You won't be making a fool of yourself. In fact—hey, watch out!"

The decayed, ancient Plymouth Voyager in front of them has veered left, crossing the double yellow line to avoid a bouncing, jagged machine part that must have fallen from the back of the jalopy truck piled high with scrap metal. The Voyager zips behind the jalopy and narrowly misses a horn-honking tractor trailer carrying doomed Perdue chickens in piled mesh crates. The truck driver is soundlessly screaming and waving a fist as Mavis slams the brakes, wanting to angle right, but there is no shoulder, just a drop-off into a drainage ditch. The hopping slab has nowhere to go but underneath the Tahoe, where it bangs like a spastic sledgehammer.

"My God!" Mavis exclaims.

"Just slow down," Charles yells. "Stay in the lane and slow down." He turns and looks out the back window. "There's nobody behind us. That thing's still jumping around, but it's twisting off the road. It looks like some kind of engine part."

Up ahead, the Voyager is passing the jalopy. As Mavis slows, the heap atop the jalopy gets smaller and smaller.

"Are we all right?" Mavis shouts. "I should've turned somewhere."

"Letting that thing hit you was the only thing to do."

"I'm still shaking. Do you think there's damage?"

"We're still driving. That's a good sign. There's a shoulder up ahead. You should pull over, and I'll have a look."

As Mavis steps out of the car, she smells gasoline. Charles is already behind the car looking at the trail of clear smelly liquid. He lays a white handkerchief on the stubbly shoulder, puts one knee on it, and cranes his head under the bumper.

"The damn thing ruptured your gas tank. But on the other hand, we're lucky. If it sparked we might've blown up. We'd be on the evening news."

"I don't believe it!" she shouts. The fuel engulfs a pothole and flows into a gully. "Are we just stuck here? I mean, I can't drive it. I can't be driving with a hole in the tank. I mean, we're still more than fifty miles from Rehoboth. It's almost 4:20 and cocktails start at six."

Charles feels buoyant. His early training, first as an information officer in the last days of Saigon and then as a city reporter for the defunct *Baltimore Evening Sun*, helped make him comfortable in situations where the script has unraveled.

"Just relax. We go back, get my car and we'll be there in

plenty of time. First, we need to report this and get the fire company out here. All this gasoline is a problem."

"Shit!" Mavis blurts, punching her left palm with her right fist. "Shit! Shit!"

So she's vulgar, too. If I wrote a speech like that, I'd be glad for a chance to miss the party. She should market it as a cure for insomnia.

Stop it, Meg. You'll make me laugh. It's close to being decent, but it doesn't matter: those politicians and educational bureaucrats wouldn't know a good speech if it bit them on the foot.

"Shit! Shit! Shit!"

Listen to her. She talks like trash. I knew she was common.

"Calm down, Mavis. We'll make a few calls and get on with it."

"I forgot my cell. It's charging on the kitchen counter. We'll have to use yours."

Charles scrunches his nose.

She doesn't know how much you hate those things. She doesn't know a thing about you.

"Well, that's a bit of a wrinkle. I left mine home. When I get away, I like to be out of touch. Otherwise, what's the point? Don't worry, though. A Good Samaritan will stop. We can even walk. I think I saw a convenience store about a mile back. Somebody'll have a phone."

Mavis has both hands up, waving at a line of approaching vehicles. The first car has a big dent in the bumper and a smashed headlight. It's a blue Subaru with two teenage boys in the front seat. Out the window flies a soda can, followed by an empty box of Kentucky Fried Chicken. Next a rumbling dump truck pulls a flatbed with a backhoe on it.

It serves you right for going out on me.

Don't be jealous. I'm just along for the ride.

"Nobody's going to stop," Mavis complains. "It never fails. As soon as I want something, they take it away."

"Maybe this'll help."

Charles takes the handkerchief from inside his jacket and

slams it inside the driver's door. Looking back down the road, he's surprised to see a new Ford Crown Victoria flashing the right blinker and pulling to the shoulder behind them.

"They're stopping," Mavis shouts, waving and smiling. A woman wearing a pill box hat sits behind the wheel. The passenger wears a flopping cowboy hat, a paintbrush mustache, and black frame glasses. "Hey! I guess I need to have more faith in people."

A Ford F-150 races past and pummels the air.

Mavis scurries toward the driver's open window.

"We had a freak occurrence. A piece of metal punctured my gas tank."

"Insurance'll cover that," the driver says. She speaks with a low grumbling sound, her tongue snaking out and licking the top of her lips. Exploded capillaries splotch her cheeks and forehead. Curly red hair bursts from beneath the pink pillbox hat. She croons in a cracked voice, "State Farm is there. Nationwide is on your side. Call GEICO direct and get a piece of the rock."

"Those bummers won't pay squat," the passenger grunts. Mavis tilts her head to listen. "You better say it was jumping around."

"It was. It—"

"We can't repair that tank," the driver moans, almost weeping. "The cat's out of the bag. The milk's spilt. The horses are out of the barn and the water's over the damn bridge."

"We have to get to Rehoboth," Mavis sputters. "Do you have a phone?"

"Get in," the passenger calls. "We're going to Rehoboth to visit the famous factory outlets. I'm Ignatius, and my sweetheart here is Brunhilda."

Mavis flings open the rear door, but Charles loops his fingers around her elbow.

"All I need is a phone," Mavis says, shaking his hand away. "Do you happen to have a cell I could use for a minute?"

"No portable bells or cells," Brunhilda laughs. "But we'll find one. Let your fingers do the walking. Reach out and touch someone. A little dab'll do you."

"Thanks a lot," Charles announces, "but we'll just wait for Triple A."

Charles yanks her elbow, trying to work her away from the car. Mavis whirls, shocked. She wriggles loose and teeters against the chassis. Has Charles lost his mind? When he goes for another grip, she pushes his hand away and slips into the back seat.

"Charles," Mavis snaps, "we never *called* Triple A. That's the problem: no phone."

She's surprised to hear the bitchy tone she regularly used on Allen.

"Make it quick," Ignatius grumbles. "Lift off is about to occur."

"Yes," Brunhilda replies, "we're late for a very important date."

"Mavis, we'd be better off waiting for the police."

She slides to the far door, her mind tilting. Time is a panting deer. The sun is eating up the sky.

"This is the best way, Charles. You wait for the police, and I'll be right back."

"Back in your arms a-gain-n," Brunhilda sings, "so satisfied."

The Crown Vic lurches forward. Charles clings to the handle. He walks to keep up with the moving car.

"Wait with me, Mavis. Get out now."

Brunhilda sings, "She's leaving on a jet plane."

"Shut the damn door!" Ignatius squawks. "The breeze is messing up her hair."

Charles is jogging now, five miles an hour, then faster.

"Charles," Mavis shouts. "Let go. You'll get hurt."

As the door pulls away, Charles sprints and flings himself inside and finds himself face down in Mavis' lap.

I told you she's a fool. Right now you could be having iced tea at your desk, feet up, watching the stock market ticker. She's rattled. She's only thinking about getting there.

You should've let her go. Serves her right. I always hated high school principals. Did I ever tell you that?

A thousand times. Leave me be. I've got to think.

It was almost transparent. Brunhilda's red wig was on crooked, and his beard sprouted here and there along his chin line in little island clumps. It was a little tougher with Ignatius, because she was hiding beneath the Panama hat.

Let this be a lesson, Charles. You can't replace me. I would never have gotten into a car with this crew.

Still on the shoulder, the Crown Vic scatters gravel and clunks from pothole to pothole. Brunhilda whips the wheel to the left, gains the blacktop, and guns it. Mavis is peering out the window. "There's a sign up ahead for a 7-Eleven. I'd slow down a little."

The speedometer edges past eighty. Charles flicks the latch and tries to lift the lock. Ignatius turns around. The glasses are crooked. And they're not even glasses—just empty black plastic frames attached to a bulbous plastic nose and a Groucho Marx mustache.

"Don't worry, Charles," she says. "You can't fall out. Our last passengers were two teenagers from Altoona, Pennsylvania. To keep them safe we set the childhood safety locks. We dropped them off in a wooded area outside Harrisburg."

"Brunhilda," Mavis calls, her voice cracking, "you missed the turn."

Charles has had enough. He lunges for the keys, but Ignatius swats his face with the back of her hand. In her right fist she wiggles a semi-automatic pistol.

Mavis screams. Charles flops back in his seat, rubbing his left eye. His contact is gone. Brunhilda beeps the horn and squeals, "I hate it when they take away the element of surprise. It never rains, but it pours. Individual results may vary."

"What is this?" Mavis asks, gasping.

"A kidnapping," Charles answers. He taps Brunhilda on the back. "Ain't that right, fella?"

Ignatius whirls, mouth chomping, gun shaking up and down. She shouts, "Bang! Bang! Bang! Don't you ever touch her again!"

Brunhilda chirps, "The life you save may be your own. A good man is hard to find. Look both ways before you leap. Actually Charles, this is a swap meet. Ignatius and I just love your outfits."

Ignatius chuckles. "I can't wait to go back and check Charles' luggage. It's a whole lot better than internet shopping. It's faster and you can see your actual colors."

"Let us out of here this instant!" Mavis yells. Her throat feels scorched. Her chest muscles clench her ribs and stifle her breath. "I'm not fooling. I have an important speech to make tonight in Rehoboth Beach."

"Okay," Brunhilda clucks, "we'll take the short cut."

Wrenching the Crown Vic off the highway, he skids along the gravel shoulder, skitters down an embankment, and careens toward a dirt road. Soon the car is swallowed by towering loblolly pines.

Mavis finds her breath, reaches forward, and shakes Brunhilda's shoulder.

"We'll have none of this. Go back. Now."

Ignatius flips all the way around, waves her pistol at Mavis' face, and sneers, "I'd stop that if I were you. You'll be making your speech to some tree roots."

"Stay calm, Mavis," Charles says. "We don't want more excitement than is necessary." He pats her hand.

"Iggy, don't they realize we came to Delaware for its famous tax-free shopping?"

"Brunhilda gets upset if she can't do her shopping."

"That's right, dear. May I borrow the death device?"

Ignatius hands him the gun but immediately wangles another one at their faces. Brunhilda lets loose a crazy loon laugh and fires four shots out the window. The bullets ping through the leaves. One gouges a four-inch strip of loblolly bark.

"I needed that." He drops the gun on his lap. "I don't just get upset." And then he roars, "I get steamed, fried, burnt, toasted, roasted, broasted, and smash-mouth *pissed*." He sighs and smiles. "Did I leave anything out, dear?"

"No. That about says it all."

You may be seeing me soon.

Stop with that, Meg. I'll have to move on these nuts. Right after the car stops. But the car is not stopping. It bumps along a rutted road crowded with trees and bramble. A hundred yards ahead, Charles sees a large lake. Some ducks and geese paddle and flap in the reflection of tall pine trees.

"You would expect," Ignatius says, "that a lake this pretty would be teeming with human activity—sailboats, chug boats, hikers, joggers."

"Progress just isn't what it used to be," Brunhilda sighs, "though I have to say, I'm a little tired of joggers. Remember that one we picked up outside of Davenport, Iowa? She was nothing but complaints. I was so glad when she finally quieted down."

Ignatius grunts. "Her jogging bra was too small for you."

"I try not to complain, dear. I just remember what my mother said, 'A stitch in time saves nine. A word to the wise is sufficient. No gain without pain. Fools make feasts and wise men eat them. So plow deep while sluggards sleep.' Mommy had a million of them."

Charles watches the gun in Ignatius' right hand. It's aimed at his chest and bobs with every rut in the washed-out road.

Whatever happens, Charles, it's all your fault. Now you see what a little excitement can do for you.

Stop, Meg. I'm trying to think.

Charles glances at Mavis. She's sitting straight up like a

schoolgirl, fingers writhing on her lap. Her eyes are plaintive, pathetic, horrified. He reaches across the seat and takes her hand. He's surprised when Mavis yanks it away and erupts, pounding the back of Ignatius's seat with both fists.

"You can't do this to us," she screams. "We're important people. I'm giving a speech, and Charles is a famous newscaster."

Brunhilda slams the brakes and screams back. "That's enough! I'm mad as hell and I can't take it anymore!"

Charles and Mavis jerk forward and flop backwards. Ignatius pins her back to the dashboard. Charles jumps at the front seat. The idea is to slam their heads together, but he manages only to whack Ignatius' Panama hat against the roof and sweep away Brunhilda's hat and wig. Ignatius fires two bullets into the rear seat cushion. By now Brunhilda is out the front door, flapping his gun and yelling, "That ain't no way to treat a lady, oh no. You're ruining the fun. This was supposed to be fun."

Brunhilda's head is a round ball shaven to a shine.

Ignatius opens Mavis' door. "Both of you out. She wants to get it over with." Though her hat is gone, Ignatius still wears the Groucho Marx glasses and rubber nose. Her hair, cut close around the sides, is curly brown on top with splotches of purple and green. "That's it. Get out slow and put your hands under your armpits. I want to see you flap your elbows. Like a chicken."

Charles and Mavis stumble on the humped ground matted with straw-like pine needles. With elbows flapping, they stumble downhill toward the lake.

"Over here," Ignatius calls, shaking the gun. She points under a black maple that hangs over the water. Charles and Mavis skid on dry, tumbling stones. With a snap, the trunk lid pops open. Brunhilda pulls out a coil of rope. "Directly under the tree. So nobody waterskiing past can see you."

Brunhilda kicks through the brown pine needles and

saunters down the pebbly hill. He looks like a bald Jackie Gleason.

"This is the moment we've all been waiting for," Brunhilda smiles.

Charles is too far away to rush them.

But at least, Charles, it'll be like coming home.

"I'm a reporter," Charles says, "and I'm curious. What's it feel like to be serial killers? I mean, what's the point? Somebody tell me."

Brunhilda swells his chest up, opening his mouth in a wide oval. "Didn't your mother teach you anything? You never ask questions of the tsarina." He raises his pistol and fires.

Mavis ducks and screams. She turns and sees Charles, his eyes squeezed shut, standing rigid and ready. He doesn't move even after it's clear that Brunhilda aimed far to his right. The bullets plunked the lake a hundred yards away. Far out in the middle, a man sits alone in a dinghy holding a fishing rod. The little man stands, looks toward them through a pair of binoculars, sits down, and starts rowing frantically toward the far shore.

Ignatius shakes her head at Brunhilda. "You went and woke up the neighbors. If we don't hurry, we'll have company calling. Okay, you two. It's time to strip. Strip!"

Ignatius fires a bullet that zings the stones to the left of Mavis' feet.

"Undress, dears," she smiles. "We have to be going."

"I'm not doing a thing," Charles says. "If you want my clothes, you'll have to take them, bloody and dirty."

"Now will you listen to that?" Ignatius laughs, scratching her head. "You're a tough guy." Out on the lake, the rowing man doesn't seem to be making any progress. He's still at least half a mile from shore. "Charles, we don't want them bloody and dirty. We want them just a little lived in. If you do things right we'll bring this thriller to an end. It's only when you don't play right that things go boom boom."

"I think it was only once, Ignatius dear. That jogging girl—she was a pesky scamp of a thing. A hussy. She made everything go screwy Louie.

"There might have been more, Iggy, but my memory isn't what it should be. Just give us the merchandise, and we will bid adieu. No curtain call, just exit to the nearest shopping center for our next free rental car."

"Pay attention to the little lady," Ignatius barks, shaking the pistol. "We got to go. Take your damn clothes off or I'll zip you both. Case closed."

Charles eyes the lake and looks at the car. Brunhilda puts the wig on his skull. With both hands, he settles the pill box hat on top.

"How do we know you won't shoot us anyway?" Charles asks.

"You don't," Ignatius snarls. "You just have to trust us."

She shoots the ground again and looks at the little man on the lake.

"Okay. Okay. Mavis, we should do what they say. What the hell."

Charles reaches for the top button of his blue shirt.

Don't you dare!

It's our best chance.

Charles unbuttons his shirt, slips it down, and tosses it toward Ignatius.

This is disgusting, Charles. She'll see you.

I want to live. Mavis does, too.

I thought you couldn't wait to see me.

It's too much, Meg. It's time you were quiet.

One by one his shoes turn in the air and land on a bed of pine needles. His cotton trousers sag to his ankles.

Mavis is not surprised to see that Charles wears blue bikini briefs, but she is shocked to see that the back of his thighs are covered with little lumps of fat. When he slips out of his briefs, Mavis can barely tell where it is. It's tucked away like a little cap amid a tuft of graying hair. Seeing Charles' fat thighs and smallish thing emboldens her. She feels her spirits lift—maybe they won't shoot them—just as a buzzing sound, like a wasp, seems to settle inside her ear. She slaps it away.

It's remarkable how quickly she undresses—shirt, bra, slacks, panties, those sheer anklet nylons—all gone, all tossed into the air. With Brunhilda pointing his gun, Ignatius gathers the goods, hustles to the trunk, and stuffs everything into a large plastic bag.

"Take the device, dear," Brunhilda says, handing the gun to Ignatius. "It's time to wrap things up. What do you think?" He picks the coiled rope from the ground. "Face to face or bum to bum?"

"Face to face is better," Ignatius says. "Okay. Hands at your sides and don't try anything funny. I'll shoot first and ask questions later."

"You got the clothes," Charles says. "What now?"

"You'll find out," Ignatius says. "Please hurry, dear. We must be going."

Across the lake the rowing man is less than a quarter mile from shore.

"Pretend you're slow dancing." And then Brunhilda croons, "Swaying to the music."

As the rope gnaws her flesh, Mavis feels the press of Charles' hands on her lower back, his chest on hers, and the scratchy tangle just below her navel. His feet lay upon her toes. Brunhilda runs round and round them, stringing the rope tighter and tighter. As the rope bites Mavis' skin, her mind drifts into another place. She's not thinking about Ignatius and the guns or Brunhilda's shiny head or the awful speech or the blizzard strafing Duluth or footsteps clomping away or the engine turning and the tires kicking gravel. Instead, she feels a settled peace fall upon her like calm rain, this feeling that she isn't going to die, not now, not soon. All she feels is how her breasts are flat against his stomach, how the rope is so tight she can't move, how she's standing stone still. She flattens her hands on his shoulder blades and scrunches her forehead just below his chin line. She can barely hear him saying how it's all right now, that the maniacs are gone, that the man across the lake will soon be calling the cops. Mavis is not really listening. Instead, she fixes her attention just below her waist where the glob of Jell-O begins to stir. It moves, stumbles, and shapes itself like a stunted thumb, pointing ever so slightly toward the sky.

THE JOLLY SEASON

"You dropped this," a woman bellowed.

Joe Cantwell turned. Her green babushka covered a nest of metal curlers. Her fat smiling face was a shade lighter than her red plaid hunting jacket. She handed him a list.

"Thanks." He stuffed it inside his brown Harris Tweed overcoat. "This is my list. I don't want to lose it."

"At least you made one," she whooped, backing through the other line of customers. "That's why I'm here. I never make 'em. Twenty shopping trips and I still haven't gotten tinsel!"

For two months now, the list had been Molly Cantwell's focus when assigning Joe his share of the shopping. Since this was Joe's first Christmas "out," it was best, she explained, that they develop a system for handling present and future Christmases. The list was symmetrical—two divorced parents shopping for an un-divorced set of twins. Not only did the list make chaos imitate order, it was extremely flexible, continually subject to change. At first, Molly had insisted that Joe pick up the Mad Scientist Dissect-an-Alien Kit for Scott and the Funwich Sandwich Factory for Zelda. Two days later, she decided she didn't want Scott sawing into rubberized alien hide, yanking out and reinserting internal organs. She was afraid he'd graduate from carving aliens to slashing cats. He had already started jabbing their tabby with sharpened sticks. Nor was it a good idea to encourage the already chubby Zelda to explore creative, high caloric innovations in sandwich design.

With a simple flick, Molly scratched out the offending entries. She substituted preschool Super Blocks for Scott and for Zelda she added Ken and Barbie dolls. In the margin, Molly noted specific ensembles: cowboy and cowgirl, doctor and nurse, fireman and starlet. She marked a double asterisk next to the astronaut Ken and Barbie costumes. Each outfit, she said, cost $17.99—a little high on the scale of things, Joe figured, but what the hell. It didn't matter if doll clothes cost slightly more than a set of plain white T-shirts and slightly less than a pair of colorful bikini briefs. Joe was loaded. Money was not one of his problems.

Making and revising the list was Joe's admission ticket. Coming up the walk to his former home, he'd take it out, look it over, and rub his chin. With Molly peeping through the curtains, he'd play the "good father" playing Santa Claus. When he stood at the door, list in hand, forehead ribbed, Molly had to let him in. There was always something to subtract, something better to add—a potentially dangerous toy, a cute gadget. The list was nothing short of a paper bridge from one way of life to the next.

During the divorce proceedings—through their respective lawyers—Joe and Molly had exchanged lists of demands as frequently as some teenagers surrender hearts. It even seemed the Christmas list was making it easier for Molly to like him again. That prospect—that Molly might like him again—had inspired him to draw up and give her a list of his own invention. Since he'd been far too busy to do any actually shopping, he'd made up a list of imaginary purchases. Soon, he'd take the list and make good. In a better world, the shopping would already be done, but he had waited and now he was stalled in line, fighting the clock.

It was the night before Christmas and all through the mall, not a creature was merry, nobody at all.

Joe's neck muscles gripped, and the guilty weight of omission pushed down on his chest like wet snow on the edge of a ragged cliff.

In Toy Fantasia, he surveyed his three loaded shopping carts and the two tricycles he kept butting forward. An immediate worry nagged him: while all the gifts he hadn't bought could have filled a room, the gifts he was about to buy might not quite fit into his new Nissan 370Z.

Joe checked his watch. It was 4:15 p.m. Seventy-five shopping minutes till Christmas gave him a little time to spare. He could drive the stuff out to the house, unload it in the garage, help trim the tree, and zoom back to Mary's by eight.

Mary Marano, a pert loan officer at First National, was his fiancée. Her parents were down from New York City, and for months she had planned a special late Christmas Eve meal—a full blown version of the Italian "Feast of the Seven Fishes." She was pulling out the stops, trying to give herself a nervous breakdown. For months, she'd worried about uncontrollable things: Could she get fresh, tender clams and calamari? Would her smelt taste like fried pencils, her shrimp scampi too tough? Would her parents finally see her as a worthwhile person?

That morning, after months of hectoring, the local fish store had come through. But she had still felt besieged by a final worry. Would he, her fiancé, be on time? He was never on time. For once in his life, he needed to be on time. Over and over he assured her he'd be on time. What did she take him for? He knew his priorities.

In his state of strained reverie, Joe happened to push the front cart a little too far. It bumped a tall elderly man holding a battery-operated train set. The red price tag said $69.99.

"Excuse me," Joe coughed.

The man surveyed Joe's mounds of boxes.

"That's some haul."

"Better late than never," Joe piped with a winning smile. He felt the old urge to spin the guy a story. "I've been out of the country for three weeks, in Argentina, doing some government work. You see, my wife's dead and my six kids have been staying with my parents. They can't get around so much anymore. I got back today and nothing's been done. Santa has to do everything at the last flipping minute."

The man turned away. Joe frowned. The guy wouldn't

cooperate. He didn't ask how the poor wife had died or the ages of all those kids or what he did for the government. The man didn't see fit to task Joe's fertile powers of invention.

There was nothing to do but stand in line. He had been inching forward for almost an hour. Though there were fifteen check-out stations, only two were in operation. It irritated him that the other line was moving so quickly and it irritated him that he was irritated. He had promised the doctor he'd avoid unnecessary irritation. One way to do that, the doctor suggested, was to focus on the good things. Joe took a fix. It was Christmas time, the jolly season. He wasn't dead. He was in love. He had two healthy, if overweight and anxious, children—twins, aged four. He made a lot of money. Just yesterday he had bought his hot new sports car.

Having run out of good things, Joe found himself slipping on the slick of the bad things. Within the past year, his father had died. His mother, after a massive stroke, languished in a nursing home, blinking at the ceiling and talking over and over about a dog named Biff that had died when she was a child. Since she hadn't known Joe or anyone else from Biff, Joe had few qualms about signing the papers that let them warehouse her. But it bothered him to visit and mumble upbeat lies about his alcoholic sister and jailbird brother. On top of it all, Joe's health could have been better. At the age of thirty-four, he had high blood pressure and high cholesterol.

Looking in the mirror at those sagging folds of flesh got him down, but not as much as the guilt he sometimes felt over Molly. His ex-wife had loved him without reservation for most of their marriage. She had suspected nothing. It was always easy for a guy who brokered real estate to get out of the house. But those overnights-out-of-the-house had done him in. She hired a detective who provided pictures—indecent, disgusting, explosive pictures. In the face of pictures, the power of story can only go so far.

Joe was now only three customers away from checkout, but

a young man at the register was having problems. The manager was there shaking his head, throwing up his hands. There was nothing he could do. The poor guy had blown his credit card limit. He would have to pay cash or write a check for the gymboree gym kit. After a lot of threats and fist-shaking, the poor guy cleared out of the store. Joe opened his wallet and took out his gold card. His fingers ran along hard edges. Its shiny face flashed with light. Joe toed a tricycle, rolling it back and forth. Staring at the card, he read his name, number, and expiration date. That was him. Or was it "he"? It didn't matter; Joseph B. Cantwell could never blow his limit. His world class card had no limit.

The sleek and low silver Nissan rumbled at the curb. The radio blared. Paul McCartney sang, "Simply Having a Wonderful Christmas Time." Sleet whipped in the wind and burned his face.

With squinting, tearing eyes, Joe stepped back and looked at the car. He had begun the operation by wedging the tricycles behind the seats and then working around them. He placed the largest boxes—like the Babe Ruth Pro Locker and the Little Tyke Big Table and Chair Set—in the back. He stuffed the crevices with boxes and more boxes: Scott's Videosmarts; Radio Control Cheetah; Road Blaster; Kid Sharp Gun and Holster Set; Power Workshop; Puke Shooter; Savage Mondo Blitzer; and Zelda's Playdoh Ghostbusters; Video Tech World Wizard; Pottery Wheel Workshop; Frog Soccer; Little Tyke Beauty Saloon; and, Pfalzgraff Cook and Serve Plate Set.

He looked at the last shopping cart. There were five more pieces to squeeze in, and he couldn't use the trunk. The trunk was loaded with Mary's gifts. No problem. He had only to size up the remaining angles. With sleet pelting him, he wedged in the Princess of Power Crystal Castle, the Master of the Universe Evil Horde Fright Zone Set, the Super Madballs Touchdown Terror Football, and two Scoot-Skate Scooter Boards. With a muffled click, the door slapped shut. He took off his soaked coat and dumped it above the hand brake. Shivering, he plopped into the leather seat, turned up the heat, wiped his face and head with wet hands, and steered through the slush.

It was 5:15. He was almost on time. In good weather, he could have made it to the house in thirty-five minutes, ripping southward around the twisting country roads, out to his former five-bedroom colonial on thirty acres of woodland. The house was out in the boonies, but thanks to his satellite dish, he had never felt isolated. In the mornings, it had been pleasant to drive to the small city where he did business, a daily opportunity to take stock of the trees and cows, to plan his activities. But that was all behind him now. He was living downtown in a singles' condo complex, where night silence was frequently ruptured by shrill screams and loud music. Joe sat and slept on rented furniture. He watched a rented TV. It was a temporary arrangement. By March, he'd be married again. He and Mary were building a house in the country a good twenty miles north of the city.

He fishtailed into traffic. Molly was expecting him at 5:30. He'd only be a little late. He smiled. All this business with the lists—he was going to get away with it.

Feeling an upsurge of lifted spirits, he slid into a convenience store lot and dashed inside. His cell phone was on his rented night table. He cursed himself for not getting the car's mobile hooked up. It would've been a cinch to give Mary a quick report—cover his flank.

There was a working pay phone next to the beer cooler.

"It's me," Joe was breathless. "I got the toys. Every flipping one. Everything's working. I might even be early. I'll dump the toys and trim the tree. I'll be out of there in no time. How long can it take to trim a goddamn tree?"

"Where are you?"

"On the road, just south of the toy store."

"I thought you were going to shop this morning. You went out explicitly to shop this morning. My mother and I've been waiting all afternoon to do the wrapping. The twins need their toys wrapped. Ripping apart the wrapping's most of the fun."

"I didn't have time this morning. The day got away from me. I called Molly about it and she said, 'Don't worry about the wrapping.' Molly loves to do the wrapping. No problem."

"Listen! I can't talk now. Mommy and I are stuffing calamari. You get moving. Hurry up and get here!"

"No sweat. Everything's under control."

Wrapping! Joe fished in his pocket for more change. Molly'll hit the roof over the wrapping.

The twins were screaming in the background.

"Molly, it's me. Merry Christmas, honey. I'm on my way. I'm calling from a pay phone. I think I lost my cell."

"The kids are wound up and I have a migraine. I thought you said you'd be here by four."

"Four? I thought I said five-thirty."

"Joe, you said four."

"I got the gifts. The car's loaded." He chuckled. "It's like riding in a sardine can."

"When you get here, unload everything in the garage. After we put the kids to bed, we can put the presents under the tree. At midnight, we'll exchange our gifts."

Joe Cantwell felt the vise-grip of panic. Molly's gifts—they were still in the store. Whatever they were, they were still in the store. "Molly, something came up. It's thrown everything off. Mary's parents had an accident. A car accident. I won't be able to stay too long. I gotta get back."

"What happened? I hope it's nothing serious."

"They're not sure what's wrong. They gotta do tests."

"How'd it happen?"

"I'll tell you when I get there. With everything that went wrong, I didn't get a chance to wrap the gifts."

"What! You told me you wrapped them last week. You said Mary helped."

"I must've meant we were going to do it last week."

In no time, Joe was driving as fast as the weather allowed. His sense of elation had been crushed by that jagged boulder in his chest. Maybe she'd simmer down by the time he got there. The quicker he arrived, the sooner he could leave. He stepped on the gas.

Out in the country, the roads were turning to ice. The sleet was changing into wet chunks of snow. Joe felt like he was driving through a tunnel. The encompassing darkness was a night cave. High beams were useless; the cave jingled with frantic flakes. Bad as it was, it was still okay. No one was out and Joe was a skilled driver in a high-performance vehicle. Even in this weather, he could eat up the miles.

Two taillights dotted the storm. In no time, Joe caught up. He downshifted to keep from climbing the back of an ancient Chevy wagon. The center line—was it broken or unbroken?—was covered. Joe was about to pass when the road snaked left in a tight curve. The Chevy fishtailed and slowed. Joe socked the wheel with the heel of his hand. Aggravation—there was aggravation at every turn. Then his thoughts braked and his stomach fell: a car came speeding at them from around the bend, high beams screaming, and crossed into Joe's lane. The Chevy swerved right and looped into a spin. To avoid a head-on crash, Joe wrenched the wheel left. Skidding on the opposite shoulder, he traveled sideways. He downshifted again and brought the wheel slowly right. The Chevy twirled twice before leaving the road and smashing headfirst into a tree. The car that had crossed the center line kept going.

In seconds, Joe Cantwell had parked and hit the flasher. Coatless, he slid down the embankment and rushed through ankle deep slush. The wet cold cut him. Afraid to look, he yanked open the door and bent over. A man in his late fifties, silver hair and thin, was chest to chest with the steering wheel. His chin topped the wheel and his forehead rested on the mangled dashboard. On the passenger's side, a dark-haired, middle-age woman had the top of her head pinned to the shattered windshield. Blood gleamed in the white snow.

"You okay?" Joe screamed. He touched the man's shoulder and slapped his cheek. He leaned in. "Hey, lady, you okay?"

They might have been dead. Joe put his hand on the guy's neck. He couldn't find a pulse, though that didn't mean much. He had a hard time finding his own pulse.

Joe stood and gathered snow from the roof of the car. The sticky blood rinsed from his hands in chunks and rills. He had to do something. He was a good fifteen minutes from Molly's. There were no houses within five miles. In this weather, he couldn't be sure he'd even make it. The hospital was back in town, more than twenty minutes away.

Joe Cantwell didn't have a choice.

Soon the toys were piled behind the wrecked car. He would have preferred to put them inside, but he couldn't get the back doors or tailgate opened. He got the man out first. Slipping and sliding, he dragged him to his car and shoved him across the back seats. The man lay open-mouthed in a semi-fetal curl. Joe put the passenger's seat all the way back, skidded to the wreck, and lifted the thin woman in one puffing motion. He carried her across his chest like a sleeping child. When he got to his car, he settled her gently down, as if putting her to bed. Her head sagged limply to the left. He draped his coat over her, tucking it around. Shivering in earnest, soaked through to his pink bikini briefs, Joe climbed in and started the engine. Neither of the passengers moved nor mumbled. He turned around, shuddering to think he was ferrying the dead.

At the emergency room, Joe Cantwell wound up wearing a green surgical outfit and hospital issue slippers. He sat in the chair beside the receptionist's desk, huddled inside a blanket, feeling like a TV Indian. The waiting room was all but empty. A young woman sat near the automatic door, staring ahead, fiddling with her fingers. Inside, her three-year-old daughter was having her stomach pumped. Earlier in the evening, she had scaled the kitchen cabinets and gotten her hands on an unsealed jar of pain killers. The red and green capsules looked like Christmas candy. At the desk, Joe was doing a poor job of answering questions.

"I have no idea who they are."

"That's okay. Didn't you jot down their license plate number?"

"Didn't think of it."

Just then a nurse came in with a wallet. "Everything's here. William and Nellie Meyer. There are numbers to call. A son and a daughter."

"Are they dead?" Joe asked. He wanted to know.

"The doctors think they'll make it. She has a fractured skull along with those lacerations and we're prepping him to remove a ruptured spleen. Both have multiple internal injuries. She's going into surgery, too. It looks, though, that we got them in time. If it wasn't for you, they'd be gone. They're lucky you were out there. I have to get back. Have a happy holiday."

"So there you are," the receptionist smiled, leaning toward him, patting his shoulder. "How does it feel to be a hero?"

The hero sized her up: pretty, brunette, thin but sinewy, a slight overbite. She'd had some bad acne once, but she was still cute, very cute. The usual urge stirred. Joe wanted to ask her for a date, but he remembered Molly and Mary. And the clock. It was well after six. He decided to act modest.

"Being a hero feels cold. I should get out of here. Can you see about the toys? Can you get the cops on the line and tell them about the toys?"

"I already did that," she smiled. "You were sitting right here when I talked to them."

"Can you check again? I need to know where to go. I mean, they were going to get them the hell out of the snow. Tell them I need to go!"

But he didn't go. First, he called Mary. She was excited and proud. Her fiancé was a hero. For good measure, Joe put the receptionist on the line to back him up. A born liar is never comfortable with God's honest truth. Mary was not upset about dinner. They'd eat at midnight if they had to.

"A stringer from the newspaper called," Joe added. "They monitor the police radio. He's on his way. He wants me to hang around and give him a few quotes."

Joe was afraid to call Molly. No matter how many receptionists, cops, or reporters he got to back him up, she would never believe him. With Mary's midnight dinner, he had plenty of time to make things right. He'd begin with the material evidence: his surgical outfit, the slippers, the blanket, the blood in the car, the bloody coat, and the snowy toys. She could call the hospital and read about it in the newspaper.

"Turn on the radio," he'd say. "I might even be on the radio."

Joe stayed at the hospital longer than he'd intended. Being a hero was a complicated, time-consuming business. First, he gassed with the reporter and then the Meyer kids showed up. They were grown, in their mid-twenties. They turned out to be twins. They talked about life as twins. By then, Joe had become good at telling the story—the headlights, the slick, the swerve. With the parents both out of surgery and upgraded to serious but stable condition, everybody was laughing. Before leaving, Joe passed around his business card.

By 8:30 he was on his way to the police station. The receptionist had phoned and said the cops had left the scene of the accident a half hour ago. When he walked into the station, he was still wrapped in the blanket. His wet clothes were in the car. His Harris Tweed was smeared with blood. He was taken to the lounge and told to wait. He poured some stale coffee and sat on a green vinyl couch. Soon, a hulking cop came in. His hair was wet. Carrying a clipboard he sat at a card table.

"Mr. Cantwell, it was a fine thing you did out there. We're going to nominate you for a Good Citizen Award."

Joe smiled. His lip twitched. He wanted out of there. The

last time he was there, he had failed the breath test.

"Thanks, Officer. I appreciate it, but I'm concerned about the toys. I left twelve hundred dollars' worth of toys in the snow. I gotta get them and get on with it. My wife is ready to kill me."

"There's a problem with the toys, Mr. Cantwell. We didn't find any. They're gone."

"Gone! You mean stolen?"

"I don't know if you can exactly say 'stolen.' The stuff was out there sitting on the side of the road. We did find this, though. It must have dropped out of your pocket."

The cop slid a crumpled wad of paper from the clipboard's metal clasp. Smoothing it out, he stood up, crossed the room, and dropped it in Joe's lap. The credit card slip was stapled to the Toy Fantasia receipt—a computerized version of the Christmas list, complete with inventory codes, prices, and tax. They never forget to add the tax.

It was ten o'clock. With headlights out, Joe Cantwell slowly negotiated the long winding driveway. He didn't want his lights to tell of his arrival. Molly didn't need a few extra minutes to gather her rage. It would be best if he appeared at the door, swaddled in a blanket, a waylaid Santa bereft of his gifts.

He parked way down by the trees and made his way from shadow to shadow, his slippers cutting a path through the drifting snow. To his left, out in the open and away from the trees, the small satellite dish was a metal totem standing alone on a white alien waste land. It stood like a sentry, cup open to the heavens and collecting signals from hundreds of stations. The house was rimmed with red and green lights. In the picture window, the Scotch pine twinkled with white lights. A lopsided angel on top had her back to the outside world. Sneaking through the snow, slipping around the foundation flower beds, Joe climbed the steps and tiptoed to the window. Under the tree were mounds of gifts, perfectly wrapped and ready. Across the room, Molly sat in a rocking chair, swaddled inside a massive Afghan. Her pretty round face sank beneath long black bangs. She was staring at the fire, holding a half-empty glass of eggnog, rocking slowly, slowly, in time with the sad-happy Christmas voice of Nat King Cole. Joe slipped and grabbed the ledge. Molly started and squinted at the window. He rolled to the side. With difficulty, Joe hoisted himself and leaned his back against the wall. His feet were numb and his hands chilled. Ten feet away, the front door locks were clattering. He pushed off and sloshed over on unsteady feet. The last lock clicked and the door squeaked open.

Joe Cantwell's plastered smile was ready-wrapped. He squeezed the crumpled kneaded receipt. He held up Exhibit A. The door yawned and his mouth opened. He was ready to let go, ring out the old, ring in the new, whatever it took to explain it all.

THE DECOMPOSING LOG

Joey Merriweather lives in the Condominium section of Squat City, a cluttered corridor jutting from a subway concourse of failing terminal shops. At the far end of Squat City, a wrecked plywood wall no longer denies access to an unfinished tunnel. Back there, among the rodent caves and abandoned excavations, Trogs eat dirt and scavenge in the sewers.

To the passing eye, Squat City looks chaotic—a poltergeist aftershock of blankets, buckets, coats, pillows, cardboard boxes, stuffed shopping bags, wooden crates, and tangled tarpaulins. But chaos (like love and fame and wealth) is relative. Squat City is actually a segregated scheme of zones, pathways, boundaries, and protocols.

At the sequestered center is Rasta Joe's Mansion, an interconnecting maze of five large ventilated crates. His expansive crawlspace world includes a living room, eatery, bedroom, study, and dumpster. His floors are sheathed with three-ply cardboard and covered with multicolored shards of tacked-down Stainmaster carpet. In the library, Rasta Joe keeps books and bongs; in the living room rests a love seat with sawed-off legs; the bedroom has a queen-size mattress; the kitchen contains a Coleman stove and an oriental table.

In the dumpster, Rasta Joe presides on a green porcelain throne. Below the seat waits a stainless-steel bucket. On the concourse side of the Mansion, a lawn chair sits under a sagging awning. On a normal day, protected from the screaming fluorescent glare, Rasta Joe will sip Jama juice, chew jerk chicken, fondle his stubble, and watch the frantic rush home race of the Upside mobs.

Every now and then, a commuter will wander near and stare.

115

Aiming to enlighten, Rasta Joe will rise and croon, "Don't worry. Be happy."

Surrounding the Mansion in a semi-circle arc are the Split Levels, a mismatched arrangement of large cardboard boxes. Here Jingo, Pinhead, Quacker, Stitch, Jolly, and Slick maintain trim cardboard patios. The boxes are mostly for sleep and storage. When a spot opens in the Split Levels, as it did with the sudden death of Trap Man, Jingo calls a council and the committee interviews applicants from the Condominium section, a respectable if unstable buffer separating the Other Half from the madding mayhem of the Ghetto.

Joey Merriweather, known to his neighbors as Huff, is among the more desirable residents of the Condominium section of Squat City. He always keeps a clean pad, folding his blankets before leaving for work, arranging his stuff in neat piles, seldom forgetting to empty his coffee can of spent butts. Though a strong candidate for upward mobility, Joey was aced out by Slick, the very first resident of Squat City to deck his condominium with plastic vegetation—holly, tulips, and carnations. It was a renovation worthy of the Split Levels. Even Rasta Joe was impressed. In no time, his crates were wreathed with shiny, rattling verdure, a color splash of red, yellow, and lavender roses. Never to be outdone, Rasta Joe extended the innovation with his silk flower statement.

It was Jingo's job to break the news.

"You didn't get the vote, my man, but you be waitin' for next time. We expectin' Quacker to hump to Florida in the spring. Then you in. Case closed."

Like the twenty or so squatters, Joey Merriweather is content to dwell in the Condominium section, nestled at night on a safe cardboard base, warm under blankets, sleeping to the open underground air. He is pleased to have left behind those Upside winter nights—the bed-of-nails misery of rumbling subway grates, the keening intensity of gusting gales, the tornado roar of downtown trains, the suffocating terror of dormitory shelters, those rooms stuffed cot-solid with the lowest degenerates, the scariest psychos, the wildest thieves. It was street anarchy rolled up tight.

For all those months, until he could get an opening, the Ghetto was better, though not by much. It encompasses the Condominium section and at night resembles a makeshift Palestinian morgue. On the linoleum, inert bodies lay scattered as if by a mortar blast. With few exceptions, the Ghetto is for losers. They come; they go. They leave their trash. They puke and pee on themselves. Every now and then, there is an uncontested rape. They steal but only from one another. A Ghetto crackhead would sooner kiss a cop's blue nose than zip the Mansion, rip the Split Levels or trash the Condos. In a former Upside life, Jingo was a Saigon MP and now he is Sheriff of Squat City. He and his deputies are always on watch. Transgressions are few and justice is swift. Joey has seen Jingo, Bo-Bo, and Quacker pound spooking snoops and dump them in the Ghetto, where they are left to prey on their own. He has seen Ghetto drecks fight one another over globs of used bubble gum. He has seen them chase rats for food. He has seen them stagger to the edge of Squat City, tumble through the torn plywood wall, and not come out. Back there, they become Trogs or maybe even food for Trogs. Joey doesn't care to find out. In the downward declension of things, he'd rather be a jumper than a Trog. With a jumper, everything is over quick. You hear the roar and see the light and maybe start to feel all bashed. But the end comes quickly. Trogs die ugly-slow in the darkest underground caves.

Joey Merriweather lives to see the day. Always. No matter how badly his chest aches or how loudly the head-hammers pound, he rises early and hurries Upside.

Today, a ruckus gags him from the depths. Hacking, wheezing, he pushes up on elbows and sees two transit cops scuffling in the Ghetto. Exhausted, he shuts his eyes and sinks.

This time they are harvesting Herbert-With-The-Crazies, an old 'Nam nut, total drug bug, and mean panhandle man. Six four and stick thin, he's got a bald head and gray bush beard. He wears puffy camouflage layers and kick-crazy combat boots. In the concourse, he stalks the weak and demands all change. Last night, Joey overheard Bo-Bo tell Goat that Herbert-With-The-Crazies socked an old lady in the face with a large stale soft pretzel.

"He even call her street-walk names, man. I tell you, Goat, that old lady be jus' as nice as my dead Mama."

"Ain't nothin'," Goat croaked. "I seed him ass-kick a schoolboy in one of them sissy Catholic uniforms. That little boy, he kicked right back. Got Herbert in the shins. Did some damage, too."

"The Herb be too long outa the bin," Bo-Bo said. "He beggin' to be bagged."

"Ain't that the truth! Yesterday, I seed him spittin' meds onto the track. One by one. Tryin' to get them in the drain."

Joey struggles from under the covers and reaches for the Marlboro Man. He slips one out and flicks his dependable Bic. Again, he opens his eyes and squints. It's all still fuzzy. Bo-Bo and Goat are standing at the edge of the Ghetto and singing, "They're coming to take me away, ha ha, they're coming to take me away." Herbert-With-The-Crazies, however, doesn't want to go. In fact, he's resisting arrest. He punches one cop. The other dings him with the club. Herbert spins around, shakes his hands free and tries to karate-kick two cops at once. A cop grabs Herbert's heel, lifts, and twists. He collapses and the cops pounce. Clubs club. Herbert-With-The-Crazies goes limp.

Joey Merriweather, huffing his smoke, stands in wobbly space. The cops grab one foot each and rake Herbert through blankets and trash, over one comatose sleeper, and into the open corridor. One cop is on the walkie-talkie.

Joey presses his fingers to his eyes and brings the big

clock into focus. It's 7:01 a.m. He's late. By now, he's usually heading east on Market, seven whole blocks, before turning south on his way to the river. There, six days a week, as dependable as the light, he takes up his broom and sweeps five loading docks, pushing into piles the butts, cans, wrappers, newspapers, and spoiled produce—the cargo rotted mess of black lettuce, wormy grapes, smashed mangoes, and bruised bananas. Sometimes, from out of the stew, he'll forage for roughage or assemble a fruit salad. From his sister's husband, dock manager Carmine de Palma, he collects twenty dollars in cash. Enough for the day's hooch and huff and enough to save for Sunday. Meals he takes mostly at the shelter— all slop and gop and whole grain crusts. When he's open to prayer, he lights upon the Mission—all that fool's gruel and knobby potatoes. The benighted converts always want to know, "Are you free in the Lord?"

When Joey Merriweather bends to fold his blanket, he feels his brain spasm. Squat City fandangos around him, all splashing colors and wiggling walls. His head constricts, thick with glue. His tongue wads: the sawdust craw is desert dry. To steady his stomach, he sucks his smoke. Water—the problem with water. Too little and too much. All over thirst and bladder burst. He reaches for his jug. Yesterday's gallon of Carlo is empty. He shakes a green jug. It sloshes. Water. He drinks enough to flatten the dust and then he wades down Condo Lane, careful to skirt the ghetto. When his legs buckle and brace, he pulls up short and takes a deeper huff. Inside, he rattles like a closet full of cracked and shattered glass.

Goat and Bo-Bo greet him.

"Hey, Huff, my man."

"How you be bein', Huff?"

Goat holds one of his large green plastic bags. He collects aluminum cans for a living. For laughs and maybe for nourishment, Goat occasionally pulls one out and snaps a wild-dog bite. He chomps and chews and makes like he swallows.

"No trains this mornin'," Bo-Bo tells Joey. "Gone be commuter hell. Upside must be a war zone."

The subway concourse is eerily empty. Only the bagel shop is open. The grates are pulled in front of the tobacco and newsstand. On a normal day, the commuters swell and clutter the concourse. It's a walled-in mass of hustling peds. Now, a lone transit cop shuffles his feet and plays with his fingers. The world is quiet. It's a remarkable thing—being able to hear.

Joey nods and steps past Bo-Bo and Goat. He needs to get to the Portable John, the city's chief concession to the ineluctable presence of Squat City. The John is tucked across the corridor, in a recessed alcove, straddled by curving iron supports that disappear into concrete slabs.

"Weather?" Out of the highest necessity, Joey Merriweather has come to master the one-word sentence.

"Don't know the weather," Goat replies, walking behind Joey. "Ain't been Upside yet. But I'll say this: the way things been, it ain't no sunny and seventy."

The City of Brotherly Love has been compressed by a January freeze. Night temperatures sink below zero. For five days now, the high has yet to reach twenty.

"Hey, Huff!" Bo-Bo calls. "Why don't ya'll bag work and kick back at my pad? Today, I be goin' exactly nowhere. Just me and my sports talk radio."

"Work!" No work, no hooch.

"One day ain't gone break you. You must got some scratch hidin' somewhere."

"*Work!*" Joey Merriweather waves them away, tugs open the John door and weaves up the step. The stench could kill a doornail.

The city shivers under glass, a glittering sheen of pimpled ice. Overnight, a misty spew of freezing rain glazed buildings, signs, poles, lights, pavements, roofs, awnings, wires, cars, and streets. The treacherous ice rink world is seized by traffic rigor mortis. A bus sits sideways against People's National Bank. In the intersection, fifteen cars nestle dent to dent. The drivers either sit surly or huddle in groups or grip handles in the slippery attempt to inspect damage. Two blocks down, stalled in gridlock, a city pick-up truck, yellow light flashing, shudders beneath a full load of rock salt.

At the top of the subway steps, Joey Merriweather clutches the railing and tries to remember if he ever knew how to skate. In front of the shoe store, a man with a spade clangs ice into slivers. A few frightened peds feel their way along plate glass, doors, brownstone, and pointed brick. One man, dressed in a fancy black overcoat and a big Russian hat, glides along on penny loafers, pushing forward one foot at a time, skating down the pavement. A woman in a long skirt and pumps barges from an apartment house door, takes two slithering steps and skids toward the street. All flapping arms and twisting torso, she is fortunate to slam a lamppost. She hugs it, cheek to squeak, and twirls down to the ground, legs all loose and heels clicking. Just now, the morning sun sneaks through the clouds and splatters the scene with sparkles. Just as quickly, the clouds close.

Joey has no idea what to do. He does not feel exactly light on his feet. The thought of slipping and falling along twelve blocks does little to quell his hammering head or untangle his twisted stomach. But the consequence is clear: no work, no hooch. Besides, it's his job to work. His father always said, "Do your job!" Today there will even be more of a job. More work, more hooch. During other winter emergencies, during last month's blizzard, in fact, Carmine let Joey fill in on union jobs. Every night, the produce comes in. Every day, it's got to get out. For three hours, Carmine let Joey drive a front loader.

He steps away from the railing. Surprisingly, he does not go flying, spinning, crashing. His floppy jogging shoes succeed in staying put. With his hands lightly pawing the air, he takes another step, sideways this time. It works and then it works again. He finds he can sidle without falling. Facing traffic, Joey

Merriweather side-winds. Left foot out and down. Stop. Right foot catches up. Stop. The outer edge of his left shoe grabs and his right foot steadies his balance. In no time, he has gone one full block. Around him, peds skitter and gasp, oblivious it seems, to Joey's discovery, this new law of Newtonian physics. Crossing the street, he steps between bumpers of stationary cars. Away from the buildings, the freezing mist settles on his baseball cap brim, which is crushed by a tied gray thermal hood. Beneath his brown, lived-in, once-upon-a-rich man Harris Tweed overcoat, two sweaters clasp his chest. Both pairs of pants straddle his hips and all three pairs of socks cling to his feet. Inside the layers, the great furnace hums. As he navigates, he feels his legs and feet go warm. His head-hurt eases; his stomach untangles. It's like taking a morning jog. Intent on his two-step shuffle, he hurries south on Fourth Street and barely notices the water gurgling up from the sewer. They will have to airdrop the water company repair crew. Joey leaves the chaos behind. So awed is he by his artful locomotion that he ignores the gaggle of black school children, freed for the day, clustering to watch the street turn into a freezing lake. As he passes, they hoot, laugh, and holler.

"The bum be ballroom dancin'."

One clapping, shimmying ten-year-old boy performs an impromptu rap.

"The white man shake/he really bake/the street be ice/like his device/he go fast/like he be—"

Through his layers, Joey barely feels the ice dart jab him in the back. He knows if he turns to hiss or snarl he will go down. The sidewalk strut requires concentration. If he can make it one more block, he will have won the day. He can then walk straight on through The Fields, an unimproved urban renewal parcel that has almost become a sports stadium, a city park, and a senior citizens center. Now, its sprawling surface is a tangled parcel of overgrown grass, burdock, pigweed, and jimson. Its edges are cluttered with mounds of clawed plastic bags, heaps of broken furniture, a display of abandoned appliances, and a mass of tinseled brown Christmas trees. Cutting through The Fields will take him right to the edge of Delaware Avenue. From there he'll have a short sidestep hop to the dock.

Safe in The Fields, the ice rink behind him, Joey straightens out. With the wind at his back, he crunches through the frozen weeds, skirting the icy landfill heaps. He lifts his foot high and bangs it through stalagmite strips that rattle, click, slither, and then crash. Beyond the abandoned refrigerator, the landscape glitters like crystal. Joey plunges on. The sky humps into rolling hills of mottled gray splashed with dabs of white. At the end of the lot, the upper floors of the dock warehouse are lost behind the deserted I-95 Expressway.

By now, Joey Merriweather feels awake and ready to work. The head-hammer is gone; his stomach merely bunches into a compliant fist of pain. He will earn an appetite for brunch. With added cash, he figures on skipping the shelter and splurging on potted meat. At the convenience store at Front and Locust, he can get some Spam, fresh Italian rolls, a box of Juicy Fruit, a bag of Doritos, and two bottles of the Bird. In the warmth of Squat City, reposing on his pad, he will make his own Thanksgiving feast.

Tangled with anticipation, Joey trips over a log and tumbles. Ice blades scrape his chilled face. He lands belly-square on a sharp rock that penetrates his take-a-moon-walk layers and punches his solar plexus. His breath leaves with a gush. He snaps his body switchblade shut, his knees cuddling his guts, his gloved hands patting his face. As he sits up, a frozen stick slices his forehead. Angry, he hoists himself to all fours, his breath still gone, and his body shaking in the hyper-wrench of asphyxiation. Gasping, he crunches backwards until his ass finds the log. He leans forward and wheezes. His pain is doing what only pain can sometimes do; it pries open the locked and rusted vault of memory. A young boy runs from his pursuers.

With the end zone looming, a hand grips his ankle. Struggling, the boy falls flat and smashes on the point of the football. That whoosh of air and then the pain. They turn him over. *Hey, Joey,* his father calls, lifting the front of the boy's padded pants. *You'll be okay. You just got the wind knocked out of you.*

Hunching atop the log, Joey Merriweather still has the wind knocked out of him. He rocks back and forth, fighting nausea, trying to suck the air. Losing his breath was like tasting death. Gradually, after lung-burst spasms, he unfolds himself and looks at the ground. He scowls; the rock he hit is not a rock but a toaster oven without a door. He shakes his head and breathes some more. The mule-kicked feeling subsides, and the stabbing forehead grinds down and dulls. He takes off a glove and dabs the wound. Flecks of blood blot his fingers. From the ground, he grabs a shredded crystal and crushes it. He brings the bits to his forehead. As the ice leeches water, he rubs in the dripping shells. The pain slinks back to its cave. Wet flecks of ice drip away. After wiping his hand on his coat, he rubs his forehead dry. He inspects his fingers. No blood. He pulls his cap to cover the scratch and is pleased to find that he has been breathing all that time.

Relieved, he lets his hand fall lightly to his side, where it barely settles on the cold log. The icy casing startles him; a log should have bark. This one has feathers. His hand travels and his fingers flutter along a knotted lump. Slowly, he tilts his head left, lowers his chin, and sees the open eyes of a man with wavy black hair. Rimmed with red, a purple hole the size of a dime dots his left temple. Like the weeds, toaster oven, streets, sidewalks, buildings, and cars, like all exposed surfaces, the man in the black tuxedo and ruffled shirt is sheathed with pimpled ice.

Retracting his hand, Joey jumps out of his skin. Crab-walk wild, he thrashes away. Around him, weeds jangle like gnomic laughter. He stares right and left to see if he is about to be arrested, finger-printed, charged, tried, and executed. He looks straight up, all ready to tell the police helicopter he didn't do it. But no one can see into this tangled bower. From where he sits, there is no warehouse, no expressway, no abandoned refrigerators, no rowhouses, no skyscrapers. It's just Joey, the ghost, and the dead man's body. There is also a weed-crushed space to his right, like some elephant rolled over on it. A trail winds off.

The dead man got dumped out in the cold. Welcome to the Upside life. He didn't even get a shuddering grate, some smelly Mission sheets or a patch of ghetto linoleum. All dressed up and no—Joey stifles the joke. He realizes the ghost can hear his thoughts, and without question the ghost hovers nearby, guarding the finished flesh like a zebra mother over her dead colt. It would not do for Joey to mock the dead. It is his be-lief that the dead are not taken away. They are not buried in the big underground. Instead, they crowd close, huddling at elbows. Joey will never say so, but every night he sleeps with his mother and father, both dead nearly forty years, taken abruptly in the car crash when he was only twelve. Even as he limped away from the wreck, he felt them clinging. He clung back. They have never gone away. They live with him in the Condominium section of Squat City.

Joey Merriweather reaches out and touches the pale blu-ish face. It is sleek with ice, not a face so much as a shield, covered on the outside and frozen within, in a state of arrest but already breaking down, already having begun to disappear. His knuckles trail over eyebrow ridges and plunk the peak of his nose. He paddles the cheek and pats the hair. Ice crumbles and flakes. Disintegration. To please the ghost, Joey offers a prayer directly to the crowded silence.

"May you find," he thinks, "the easeful repose of life eter-nal. Mom and Dad, please help steady this newborn ghost."

"Who?" Joey blurts, scattering the silence. As much as he'd like to, he cannot bring himself to speak whole gobs to the dead man's body. The ghost already knows his thoughts, hears the whole question, but the murdered man's body cannot hear.

"Search."

Joey fans his hands across the chest and finds a bulge above the heart. He lifts the lapels and breaks the ice. He slithers his hand inside, afraid of touching the feathers. He feels the lump and takes it out. The wallet has credit cards and pictures and a driver's license behind a plastic sheath. Joey turns it to the side and squints.

James P. Pierce. 1868 Woodrow Lane, Radnor, PA.

Jimmy Pierce. Downside, he would need a handle. Jimmy is for Pierce and P. is for Pistol.

"Hey, Huff!" Goat calls. "Who you got there?"

"Pistol."

"He be stiff and straight all right, a real son of a gun."

Joey removes a bunch of green from the wallet and fans it.

By now, the ground chill has seeped through the layers and shivers his bones. With a creaky push, he gets to all fours and stands up. He slips the wallet into his pocket, puts his glove back on and looks up.

Without speaking, he informs the ghost, "Don't worry. I'll take good care of the Pistol." And then, with a wild thrilling defiance of the consequences, he looks down, draws a breath, and lets his voice go. His voice is cracked and hoarse, but his words are refined, precise.

"Mr. Pierce, you are in quite a predicament, almost past help. But I'll help. I'll see to it that your day improves."

It's been more than a decade since Joey Merriweather has spoken on the telephone. It's not a matter of hating speech— he loved and loves words. Rather, he fears the dissipation of his soul. Years ago, at the college where he taught, he ripped away the veils and achieved synthesis: Spirit is the Creator and contains life within itself. The soul is breath—Atman—and breath effuses from the omphalos, the deep center, the eternal circle. If the Word became Flesh, then Spirit is coextensive with words. Talk is so much dissipation. He understood why the church mystics breathed with God and ghosts in silence. Professor Merriweather's brilliance was in his peculiar method of atonement: to smoke a cigarette was—is—to relinquish the self in a burnt offering, exhaled breath could carry unspoken words back to Spirit. The University Administration did not see the poignancy of his one-word lectures and his hour-long smoking at the podium. His wife refused to stay married to silence and smoke. He opted out, gratefully. But now is a problem; here is a telephone, and back there wait the ghost and Pistol.

Joey lifts the receiver and smacks the ice from the keyboard. He pauses. He promised the ghost and owes Pistol. He squints and pushes 9-1-1.

"City emergency," a woman says. "Speak clearly, please."

He freezes to the sound. Has his ex-wife become an operator?

"Is anybody there?"

No. There are other women in the world. "Dead!" Joey mumbles.

"Pardon me? I can't help you if you don't speak up. Did you say someone is dead?"

"Fields."

Inside the furnace, pressure builds. Joey sweats. He wants to give it up and scurry Downside.

"Who is Fields? Is Fields dead? Please, sir, speak up! Otherwise, I will have to cut you off."

"Anima mundi," he sputters. It's as close as he gets to an explanation. He's trying to say he doesn't want to lose his soul. He breathes hard.

"Are you all right, sir?"

The wind shakes the open booth. The chill pierces his core. It's the ghost. The ghost followed him to see how he would do and now the ghost is jabbing him. Pierce is Pistol and Pistol is Pierce. "All right, then, I'll do it," he shouts. Fighting tears, he surrenders. "There's a dead man left like a decomposing log in the middle of The Fields."

"What fields, sir?"

Joey sighs, exasperated. His students were the same way. Everybody wants more than they need.

"The undeveloped acreage near the waterfront, below Locust. Walking to work, I tripped over James P. Pierce. He was rushed into eternity, before schedule, execution style, as the newspapers say. He's there. You have to get them to get him. I can't do any more. I already said too much, but I made a promise to Pistol's ghost. I'll take good care of his personal effects."

The receiver slips from his fingers into the cradle. Now, he will need to smoke two extra packs for the next forty days and forty nights. His stomach twists into a walnut. Joey wants to drink.

"Yo! Hey, Joe!"

He turns. Across the street, at the edge of the parking lot, Carmine stands inside a great parka. He looks like an Eskimo.

"More than half the crew ain't in. I need you, Joe. You can work the forklift."

Joey Merriweather waves to his brother-in-law. He points toward the next corner. "Busy."

Facing Carmine, Joey sidesteps up the block. Keeping pace, slipping on mincing steps, Carmine waves his hands.

"What do you mean, busy? There ain't a car in sight. Where the hell you going? I need you today. It's time to wash my back."

Pushed along by the gusting ghost, Joey fingers the wallet.

"Minute!" he shouts and waves his left index finger.

"By the way, who the hell were you talking to? I thought you didn't talk no more."

Joey reaches the mailbox and yanks the handle. As he drops the wallet into darkness, he feels the ghost leave. It hurries back to Pistol. Somewhere in the city sirens are singing.

"Come on! Get over here! Joe, listen, I need you. You can work as many hours as you want. I'll pay you double."

He sidles across the street.

Carmine grabs his elbow. They sidestep and slip-slide across the parking lot.

"Let's move it. We got all this fruit to unload. I got an idea, Joe. Let me know what you think. At lunch, now that you're talking, why don't you settle down in my office and give Patsy a call? She'd love to hear from you. She worries, is all. She won't show up again and try to drag you into the car. I promise. She just wants to talk to you. You don't have to say much. Just say hello. At lunch, we'll kick back and give her a ring. How about it, buddy? Just call and say hello. What do you got to lose?"

YOUNG MR. MOYEN

Young Mr. Moyen came forth at sunset, tripped over the threshold, and stumbled down three flaked rickety front steps to the cracked slanted sidewalk. Felicia put out a hand to steady him, but when his feet tangled, he flew beyond her, not stopping till his shoulder struck the lamppost and he twirled like an antic child, settling to the curb, legs flat out. When he looked up, he saw the deep folds of Felicia's pink and green peasant dress flapping his way. He got to his knees, clutched the knobs of her hips, and pulled himself up. When he lost his grip, his face plunged between her legs. The scent of mothballs and Sweet Honesty perfume almost made him gag. With a determined gasp, he pushed himself up, his chin riding the chubby slope of her abdomen and snapping across the wire-framed mound. Mr. Moyen got back on his feet. Thin and willowy, he was four inches shorter than his three months' bride.

"It's a bad sign," Felicia said, "this falling all over yourself. If you're so exhausted, you should just stay home."

Mr. Moyen worked as a washing machine operator in the southwest Philadelphia General Electric plant. All day, with the help of a hydraulic platform and a hand operated crane, he loaded machine parts and casings on metal trees. They were conveyed along an elliptical track where they were washed, dried, and painted. When the pieces came back, Mr. Moyen put them on wooden skids. Lenny, the shop steward, took them away on a front loader.

"I can't miss the union meeting. I'm expected."

"It's the right time of the month." Felicia's smile seemed to waver, as if she were reminded of an embarrassing complication. "In twenty minutes we could be trying. When you're done, you can sleep and have nothing but nice dreams."

"The best dream," Mr. Moyen fretted, "is no dream at all. I hate finding myself in strange places, locked in a box or caught in an alley with dark figures closing in around me. When it happens, I know I'm dreaming. I want to wake up but can't."

"That's why you need sleep." This time her smile was full and forthright. "It never takes you long. Stay with me, especially tonight. Please. It's time."

Mr. Moyen's groin tightened. In their room's dim light he could see what was ahead of him— breasts sagging to her waist, squatting astraddle, pushing down as if to break him in two. Her eyes would be squeezed shut and the three pink ribbons that normally kept her thick brown hair wrapped in a bun would shake like a hanging coil of electrified garter snakes.

"I have to go, especially tonight. I gave my word to Lenny." He pulled away, stumbling. With a lift of his toes, Mr. Moyen kissed his lawful wife lightly on the forehead. "Trust me. It's all about the future."

"Well, then," Felicia sighed, "I shouldn't be holding you back."

"Just keep the faith and don't forget to pray. Jesus."

Mr. Moyen turned and hastened down the sidewalk, conscious of neighbor eyes staring from both sides of the sloped street. Perhaps they could see behind his impassive face to the guilt that itched like a troublesome rash. His lies to Felicia were luminous beams shooting from his heart, attracting the smiling gaze of old hunched Martha Carrier. She was watering pink petunias in large stone pots. In her late seventies, the pious Mrs. Carrier worked as a crossing guard at the corner of Hathorne Street. Every afternoon she handed lollipops to school-weary children. Mr. Moyen escaped her gaze lest she glimpse how this quiet neighbor boy—no, this young good man—was not simply out for an evening stroll but in pursuit of terrible intentions.

Mr. Proctor for one didn't seem to notice anything unusual about his neighbor. He was a squat man in his fifties. He had a pleasant face and wore a flopping green golfer's hat. He was holding the leash of his black Labrador retriever, Danforth, who sniffed the base of a telephone pole. A retired master carpenter, Mr. Proctor spent many free hours framing houses for Habitat for Humanity. He had yet to speak to Mr. Moyen about anything other than Phillies' games.

"Can you believe the bums?" Mr. Proctor cheerfully hollered. "Up by three in the ninth and they let it get away. The team's going straight to hell."

Danforth lifted his leg and sprayed.

Mr. Moyen offered a foolish thumbs-up. He had meant to smile, but as he hurried down the rowhouse canyon he merely grunted. He caught the eye of Ann Hibbins, Felicia's best friend, who was sitting on her porch. In the windup swing, her son glided back and forth, his chubby hands smacking the tray and scattering Cheerios.

"Thank God for Mr. Corey," Ann said. "The whole block could have burned."

Two doors down, a brick rowhouse was boarded up, a consequence of yesterday's fire. With cigar in hand, Mr. Hale had fallen asleep on his couch. He crawled out the front door before smoke and flames gutted the interior. The cinderblock firewall kept the adjoining houses from becoming involved, a situation abetted by the heroic efforts of Giles Corey. When the fire broke out, he had been washing his maroon Taurus on the sidewalk. He climbed atop his porch and in defiance of smoke, flames, and common sense, he hosed his neighbor's roof until the fire engines arrived.

"I can't talk," Mr. Moyen mumbled. "I'm running late. Felicia said she'd call you in a few minutes."

Mr. Corey was sitting on his stoop. He waved to Mr. Moyen,

who tucked his chin inside his shirt and nodded curtly. He received a shouted greeting from Thomas Putnam, who was across the street re-screening his front porch. Mr. Putnam managed an auto parts store, but his great passion was coaching Little League sports. His three sons were grown and gone, but year after year he coached baseball, soccer, basketball, football, and roller hockey. He was a permanent deacon at St. Francis Assisi, parish coordinator for the annual Catholic Charities Appeal, and president of the Liturgical Council. With sliding stomach and gurgling bowels, Mr. Moyen waved to Mr. Putnam, who seemed like he wanted to speak, perhaps to ask again if Mr. Moyen would be so kind as to cover door-to-door solicitations for Hathorne Street and one or two adjacent blocks.

Fortunately, Mr. Moyen reached the corner and sneaked a quick look behind. Felicia was still standing on the sidewalk, reaching a black hand into the darkening air. She might have been throwing a kiss or waving him home, but he stepped around the corner into long shadows, which blotted out the pink and purple sky. With his back turned against his street, the church, convent, and rectory, he traveled eastward along the uneven cracked and weedy sidewalk toward the little cluster of shops that gave the Darby trolley loop its deceptive glow of life.

Mr. Moyen looked at his watch—he was five minutes late—but he had not heard a trolley's departing rumble. The rusted poles circling the tracks were black spears stabbing the sky. The sagging wires seemed the shoddy abandoned work of a large Hollywood spider. The Plexiglas shelter was deserted. It stank of urine and was defaced by graffiti and drawings. *Peggy Sue goon fuck you to.* A pencil-like penis impaled a stick woman's forehead. Plastic cups, empty soda cans, smashed french fries and mustard-stained wrappers littered the cindered ground. With slouching shoulders, Mr. Moyen plopped on the gray plastic bench and patted the two tokens in the right front pocket of his brown corduroy pants. His eyes happened upon a piece of the street between the shiny tracks. Layers of asphalt had been worn down or hacked away, exposing a patch of cobblestone that must've dated to the early twentieth century. Back then, Darby was a thriving suburb with nothing to suggest it would become a ruinous borough in desperate need of a catastrophic tornado and the ensuing balm of Federal disaster relief.

"You're a little late, my friend. When I first arrived I felt just as Felicia feels: I didn't think you'd be coming. But I'm pleased to see you've gotten over any apparent misgivings."

Mr. Moyen was startled to find himself seated hip to hip with a smiling grave-faced man. As nearly as one might guess, the stranger was about fifty years old, dressed in brown loose-fitting work clothes, and looking enough like Mr. Moyen to pass for a near relation, perhaps even his father.

"Felicia held me up," Mr. Moyen muttered, his voice quavering.

Despite his humble clothing, the stranger possessed a cosmopolite ease that would have served him well at a presidential reception.

"Good wives always hold up their good men," the stranger smiled, cocking his ear. "But no matter, the trolley is approaching. It, too, is a little late."

At first, Mr. Moyen heard nothing, but then from around the bend came the grating rattle of a decrepit SEPTA trolley. As the single headlight swayed into view and caught them in its beam, the trolley turned into the loop. The whistling wheels sounded like a keening witch's cry. The trolley thumped, banged, and screeched to a stop. From out of the rear door lumbered a massive black woman with closely cut hair. She was dragging a stuffed carry-all bag. The sagging flab of her upper arm jiggled.

The stranger stood and tugged Mr. Moyen's elbow.

"Felicia's not feeling well," Mr. Moyen stammered, clenching the sharp underside of the bench. "It's her stomach. She can't keep anything down."

The stranger rose and took the first step toward the trolley's open front door.

"These stomach conditions," he smiled, "pass quickly away. Who knows? Even as we speak, she may be bustling about, getting ready for a pleasant moonlight stroll."

"I don't think so. Felicia's afraid of the night and would never go out alone."

The stranger smiled, "No one going out at night is ever truly alone."

Mr. Moyen shook his head and climbed the steps, dropping his token into the slot. The stranger followed, cheerfully greeting the hawk-nosed driver and directing Mr. Moyen toward the narrow seat behind the rear door.

"I noticed you didn't pay," Mr. Moyen remarked as he slid into the cramped seat. "I have another token if you need it."

"It's kind of you to offer, but you should save your last token for the ride back home. My special pass gives me unlimited access. I'm a frequent traveler on these lines. Not fifteen minutes ago, I was speaking with two of our new members at the Broad and Olney subway station."

The trolley lurched forward and the coffee shop, now darkened to blue by the scratched tinted glass, seemed to float and pulse in the air. The wheels shrieked on the curve and the trolley rattled toward Darby's virtually defunct business district. Outside a pawn shop stood three black men and two white men. Handing a bagged bottle back and forth, they were laughing and talking. As the trolley passed the open door of a ramshackle taproom, Mr. Moyen pressed his nose to the glass and perceived shadowy, ghost-like figures moving in the uncertain light. He caught a glimpse, if such a thing were possible, of Sister Maria Cloyse, principal of St. Francis Assisi School, swigging from a bottle and shaking her billowing midriff in a modestly obscene manner. Mr. Moyen bent his head farther back to catch a second look, but the open door was too far behind him. On the pavement, beneath the awning of a secondhand clothing store, a beggar sat on a milk crate surrounded by three filthy backpacks and a rolled-up sleeping bag. Two policemen stood over him. One was nudging the beggar's ribs with a night stick. Behind them, a fat white woman with curly black hair brought a steel mesh grate crashing to the pavement. The clanging metal rang like a slammed cell door. It stirred Mr. Moyen's conscience.

"Well, sir, I think I've gone far enough. I've been giving the whole thing a lot of thought, and I'm not quite ready to make the kind of commitment your cause deserves."

"Is that right?" the stranger replied, smiling. "Perhaps we should discuss it as we go. Tell me everything you feel. No scruple should be ignored."

"I don't want to be caught—"

"It's a consideration, surely, but you must remember we have influential friends in a host of influential positions. Police can be—"

"I'm not concerned with the police so much. I was wondering about being caught up with"—and here he sighed—"such a crowd. What if someone I know sees me?"

"To such a concern, I can only say how well met the two—the many—of you would be. Membership is far more extensive than you can imagine. Almost everywhere we have compatriots, companions, associates, colleagues. The same concerns that bring you out tonight have brought others before you and will bring many more tomorrow and tomorrow and tomorrow." He shrugged. "It's little more than a coven of friends with significant work to do."

"But I'll be the first of my family to go to such lengths. How could I look—"

The stranger's lips wriggled like a snake and twisted into a sardonic smile. "Forgive me for interrupting, but I knew your father as well as your grandfather. Over the years, they accompanied me on many an errand. Both were members in good standing. In fact, your father and I first did business of a delicate sort when you were no more than four or five years old. It was secret little matter involving rags and gasoline. And some years before that necessary trifle, I helped your grandfather when a questionable, dark-skinned person was taken for a long car ride. When we returned from the forest, it was with a lighter load."

The trolley was stopped in front of a boarded-up TV repair shop. Five or six passengers clunked on. Mr. Moyen was startled to find the trolley almost packed. It had left Darby, crossed Cobbs Creek and had already gone a few blocks into southwest Philadelphia. When the trolley shunted forward, Mr. Moyen tugged the stranger's sleeve.

"I can't speak for my grandfather, but I never heard my father mention anything like that. For twenty years, before he died, he was the town magistrate. I never knew him to do a secret thing."

"That's quite an insinuating answer," the stranger laughed. "Let me put it this way. There's always more to a father than meets a child's eye. And as you already know, at least for a time, all depends on secrecy. Oh, my! What have we here? She really does move with surprising speed. Would you excuse me for a second?"

They had arrived at the next corner. A boisterous clutch of people pushed and clattered up the steps. The fare box rattled. The air was rifled with confused voices and anxious squeals. A sudden scream morphed into raucous laughter. The stranger worked his way up the aisle, exchanging greetings along the way, and reached a white-haired old lady, who sat behind the driver in one of those long sideways seats. The head and profile closely resembled Mrs. Martha Carrier. Mr. Moyen alternately ducked his head to avoid detection and strained his neck sideways to steal a surreptitious look. But standing passengers obstructed his view. When Mr. Moyen saw the stranger pointing in his direction and the old lady looking his way, smiling, nodding, he slumped in his seat and stared out the window. He strained to see through the blue glass and for a second or two he glimpsed a darkened alley and a man resembling Mr. Proctor, his Phillies' cap ajar, beating the ribs of a large black Labrador retriever with a small baseball bat. As the trolley moved along, Mr. Moyen's curiosity gave way to a new disturbance. Among a crowd of young men emerged someone who looked like gray-haired, gentle Thomas Putnam. He was holding hands with a tall thin black man, who wore a tight red Spandex jump suit and a blond fright wig. As Mr. Moyen squinted, Thomas Putnam licked his lips, hugged his companion, and buried his tongue inside the man's ear. In an instant this scene was lost behind a double-parked Budweiser truck. Mr. Moyen looked to the front of the trolley and was startled to find no trace of the stranger. Nor could he detect among the bobbing heads the white hair of good Martha Carrier. On the side seat behind the driver now slouched a chunky young black man wearing a purple do-rag and a blue Iverson jersey.

Feeling relieved, his escape route before him, Mr. Moyen stood up, swung around the pole and stepped into the well of the rear door. He pulled the cord and waited for the door to open. Outside the careening trolley, there were people, cars, and buildings rushing by in a blue whoosh. He looked at every head on the trolley and assured himself that the stranger had somehow disappeared. Unfortunately, the trolley was speeding along a curved stretch of track toward the cavernous mouth of the 40th Street tunnel. Mr. Moyen was heading underground and would have to wait until the next stop at 34th Street. Then he could get off, climb to the street, cross over, go down the steps and use his last token to catch the next westbound trolley.

Outside the speeding trolley loomed the blackness of darkness, relieved only by an occasional dull bulb that seemed to

rip past in the opposite direction. The window reflected Mr.
Moyen's gaunt face and ribbed forehead. Stricken, he looked
away and into the eyes of an old white-haired woman smiling
at him from across the aisle. She was saying the rosary. With
a spurt as sudden as a ruptured aorta, he imagined taking the
rosary and wrapping it around her throat till her neck bulged
and blackened. Blinking three times to erase the repulsive
specter, Mr. Moyen slipped all the way down into the exit well
and yanked the cord four quick times. From the front of the
trolley snarled the driver's raspy yowl, "Hey, mister, I'm gettin'
rid of you as fast as I can."

A water wash of light engulfed the trolley, which braked
hard. The bi-fold doors flapped open and Mr. Moyen stepped
onto the soiled concrete platform. As the trolley clattered
away, he felt like cursing the driver, but without thinking,
he pressed his belly button and watched the trolley explode,
filling the tunnel with an orange and yellow fireball. Frightened, he slapped the side of his face, blinked twice, and was
surprised to see the trolley's rear red lights twinkle and disappear around a bend. He walked toward the stairs. On the wall
between a vodka ad and a *Broadway is Best* poster hung a gallery
of pictorial obscenities—a Cubist collage bearing a closer re-
semblance to spears, blimps, watermelons, and slashes than to
any human sex organ. With heavy tread, he scaled the steep
and grimy stairs, the dull ceiling light playing host to attacking
bug swarms and an expansive spider web. A huge hairy black
blot careened toward three moving figures. Mr. Moyen slowed
and was amazed to see miniature versions of his mailman
Frank Parris, his barber Zeke Cheever, and his pastor Father
Murdock. They were little human bodies ensnared in the trap,
their eyes wide and their mouths working vigorously without
making a sound. Mr. Moyen picked up a yellowed newspaper
and wadded it into a bat. When he turned, the little writhing
faces were either gone or Mr. Moyen was staring at another
part of the web. Nevertheless, he slashed the netting with

furious sweeping motions. Soon he was sawing nothing but air. With a panicky gasp, he tossed the newspaper and ran up from the underground.

When he reached the street, he found himself immersed in a mob of laughing, screaming people. They were all heading eastward as if toward a baseball game, a rock concert, or a public execution. Mr. Moyen tried to push his way north and cross the street, but a human freshet swept him along. In the crush, his feet left the ground and his body was borne sideways. Soon, he feared, he'd fall through some gap and be trampled by a thousand hurrying feet. He had no choice but to turn and ride the stream. The mob was so tightly packed that he could not bring down his arms. He could do nothing but fan the air before him. Streetlamps were out and he moved through a darkened world, as dark as a moiling night wilderness—the fierce cries of four-legged beasts converging into a vicious carnival murmur, where mirth was little more than a mask for malice. Screams and laughter raked the humid air. Mr. Moyen's arms tired. In letting them sag, he happened to touch a woman's pimpled neck. Her skin was hot and scaly—a scabrous sweaty oily sheen. His hands snapped away as if bitten, but not soon enough. The hag's head swiveled in an abrupt contortion. In the shimmer of light cast from a second story window, she showed snapping teeth. Her tongue was pierced and plugged by a silver ball. Mr. Moyen started to speak, but her spewed words chopped into him like an axe.

"Shit sucker scum. Bad Jermaine gone cut you up."

Mr. Moyen wanted to dig his fingernails into her eyes, but he was distracted by a colliding clutch of hands rifling his pockets, jabbing his ass, squeezing his balls. With a twig-snapping wrench, someone pinched his penis. Staggered by pain, Mr. Moyen stumbled to the right, slipped through an open space and tumbled against a granite building. He bunched into a crevice and watched the mob flow past with the slow pace of cows hoofing toward slaughter. He would wait here for the street to clear. Then he would make his way back to the underground. Even at this hour, the trolleys never took more than twenty minutes to arrive, not unless there was a power failure, a tunnel fire, or a suicidal jumper.

Mr. Moyen nestled further into the wall and lifted himself so he could better watch the mobbed sea of bobbing human heads. As another slash of light cut the air from a room somewhere above, it fell like a spotlight on the laughing head of a woman who resembled Felicia more in feature than expression. This woman's shoulders were squeezed into a low-cut black leather tee shirt and her breasts seem to spill out like bulging mounds of detonated earth. In the back of her thick hair was a single pink ribbon. Next to her appeared the face of Ann Hibbins, her mouth painted with a clown-like oval of blood red lipstick. After hugging Felicia and kneading her breasts, Ann buried her painted mouth in Felicia's neck like a hatchet. Ann's lithe fingers seemed electrified and her lips were mechanized suction cups. With a twisting spasm, Felicia threw back her head, let out what might have been an orgasmic howl and tried to lick the side of Ann's face. Mr. Moyen was stunned. It was like waking up in a darkened hotel room, the blue TV light still flashing, and finding his very own wife writhing naked on the screen, hands clutching the bars of a prison cell as she was taken from behind by a masked man. Mr. Moyen could neither turn off the picture nor adjust the sound. He could only squint to get a better look.

Slowly, Ann and Felicia drifted out of sight. Mr. Moyen was now looking at the backs of their heads. After another stupefied instant, he squeezed his right hand over his heart. Enraged, he bellowed, "Felicia! Turn back!"

In such an uproar, the woman, whoever she was, could not possibly have heard his voice. Nevertheless, she turned. Her eyes were incandescent and wild, lit by a kind of jovial madness, a party fever fury. When Mr. Moyen recognized what might have been the hand-shaped birthmark on her left cheek, he felt then that his heart was gone forever. In its place was lodged a whole cold potato—lumped, brown, dirty, frizzled with wiry, sprouting weeds. He pictured himself pushing Felicia out of their mortgaged house, down the front steps to the pavement, and then after two fierce kicks, she would be on her way, out of his life forever. She'd never squat on him, never use her down-driving weight to try and cut him in two.

With Ann Hibbins still sucking the side of her throat and her hands still fondling her breasts, Felicia wriggled out of control, though she seemed suddenly quite deliberate when she brought her right hand to her mouth, spat heavily into her cupped palm and flung the hocking load like a Frisbee toward his appalled face. As Mr. Moyen watched the gob rise in the air and descend toward him, a fist smashed the side of his face and he slithered down the wall. By the time he pushed to his feet and steadied himself, Felicia was gone.

Without thinking, though spurred by a rage to catch up, he plunged into the mob and was amazed by how quickly he made his way forward. A path seemed to open at every point. Mr. Moyen hurried as if propelled by great gusts of wind. He had every intention of catching Felicia and casting her off, but not before he found a rock or a brick and brought it down atop the skull of the treacherous Ann Hibbins.

As he raced and stumbled, he became conscious of being cheered. He heard the applause and felt numerous hands slapping his back. The way opened even more and he ran harder, no longer concerned about catching a westbound trolley but increasingly apprehensive about the two sheets of paper folded in the left rear pocket of his brown pants. The original venue, he recalled, had been the storage area of the massive post office at 30th and Market, but at the last minute the location had shifted to the main quad of a nearby university. His path now took him through a tree-shaded break between enormous buildings. The branches flailed like attacking arms and accusatory fingers.

Under floodlights, the stage was nearly empty, but the audience was a crush of cheering people. As Mr. Moyen hurried along the jostling perimeter, the applause increased, and he could almost have sworn that he saw his father—dead five years—carry a chair across the back of the stage. In the wings of the flatbed stage were three old-fashioned nuns in billowing black habits, white wimples, and black veils. As he stumbled up the steps, Mr. Moyen saw the smiling stranger remove the microphone from the stand, the cord twisting and whipping like a tortured eel. In the shadows of the rear of the stage, partly hidden by curtains, he thought he saw a woman with wild bushy hair, though her face was obscured by a man in a turban, who held a long stick balled at its point with fire. Over and over, as if to practice, he swallowed the flame. Climbing over the top step, Mr. Moyen tripped, tumbling forward, but strong, unseen hands steadied him. As he wobbled to center stage the spotlights were blinding.

Offering the microphone, the stranger leaned toward him and whispered, "Once we were sure you were coming, the word got out and not a single member wanted to miss the convocation. This interest derives partly from the high esteem in which your family is held and partly by the passion you so clearly possess for doing our work. And it's right for you to begin this way—with the speech you've worked on for so long—here, center stage. For so long, deep within yourself, you have wanted to become one of us and now as soon as you catch your breath, you may commence."

Mr. Moyen took the microphone in his right hand and tried to put it back on the stand. Feedback serrated the air. He reached into his back pocket and pulled out the quarter-folded sheets of paper and tried to arrange them on the podium. His mind, usually muddy and slow, a thick mire, had become almost luminous. He remembered the acceptance speech he had worked on for weeks. Anytime Felicia was out shopping or down in the basement ironing clothes, he pulled out his secreted text and worked over the words—about how happy he was to join, how he looked forward to carrying out certain attacks central to their common cause. He wanted especially to destroy all churches and advance the death of all belief. It was his special mission to show the credulous world how God was nothing more than a fool's fond dream. It was time to smash every fragile box. Everything was based on sham: civic duty, pennies for the Pope, the forty-hour work week, taxation with representation, raffle tickets for dying children. The truth of nothing was the fact of everything. It made him want to laugh.

With the feedback whining and roaring, Mr. Moyen began to read his speech. Every single word was abruptly snarled by whirring screeches. The crowd groaned. They were waiting, perhaps, for him to propel them into action, to stir up the flames, to initiate the great stadium wave of focused destruction. He was ready to shout it, fist balled. Tonight, for starters, they would march downtown and take over and burn the Cathedral of Saints Peter and Paul. He was ready to give the word, but the microphone seemed to be attacking him, bickering back with a satanic squeal.

From the far right appeared a legion of flashing lights. Riot police were overtaking the quad. Wearing wire mesh masks and shiny white helmets, they were swinging clubs and beating back the dispersing crowd. Mobs of people disappeared into hedges, shadows, and arched doorways. Still tethered to the microphone, Mr. Moyen stood on the stage alone. The stranger was no longer beside him. The fire-eater was hustling down the steps. When a tear gas canister exploded stage left, Mr. Moyen dropped the pulsing microphone and ran away on shaky legs. He slid down the steps, skittering across the lawn toward a clump of trees. Behind him three policemen dragged two kicking women across the pavement. He heard gunfire and bullets sizzling through leaves. One cop swung his club and whacked a blond woman on the side of the head. When she fell, the cop turned and stared directly at Mr. Moyen. The cop called to him and started jogging his way, stick raised. Mr. Moyen turned and fled. With flailing arms, he crashed through a row of sticker bushes. Close behind him were shouts. Something large was thrashing in the bramble. A terrified Mr. Moyen stumbled forward and glimpsed an opening in a brick wall. Scratched and bleeding, he got through the door and sprinted into a dark stand of trees, trying to reach the deepest darkness ahead. He was almost there, but as he turned around to see if anyone was following him, he smashed his head against the low-lying limb of a hundred-year-old oak. The blow staggered him, though he didn't fall. He shook his head and wobbled, feeling his way along the branches, eyes shut, head screaming, pushing forward, engulfed by darkness and then not feeling anything until his earth-slapping feet gave way and his face smashed down to the ground. Almost immediately, or so it seemed, a hand was shaking his shoulder. Mr. Moyen felt the slick wooden bench beneath him as he opened his eyes. His head wobbled. Everything was wet and cold.

"That's a pretty mean looking lump on the side of your head," Mr. Proctor said, pushing back the brim of his Phillies' cap. "What happened? Did you get mugged? I heard on the news there was some kind of riot in West Philly last night. Those anarchy nuts were at it again, stirring up trouble on the Penn campus. They almost got the ringleader, a guy who calls himself Brown. You weren't anywhere near there, were you?"

Mr. Moyen didn't answer. He was sitting in the Plexiglas shelter in the Darby loop. Early morning light painted the eastern sky with pink pastels. In his right hand, he squeezed two crumpled, quarter-folded sheets of paper. They were dabbed with blood.

"When you got off the trolley, I was having breakfast in Bud's. I figured you had gotten overtime at the plant. I looked again and you were still here. It's been more than fifteen minutes. Hey, your face is all scratched." He pulled out a cell phone. "You want me to call your wife. What's the number?"

"There's no good on earth."

"Yeah, that's their slogan, the sick turkeys."

"The police."

"I can call them, too. But your wife will want to know. I saw her standing at the door. She looked tired, like she'd been up all night. When she gets a look at you, she'll want to call an ambulance."

"My Felicia's gone. Mr. Brown will tell you."

Mr. Proctor nodded and patted his shoulder.

"Concussion. It makes you talk crazy. Did the mugger get your wallet?" Mr. Proctor flipped open his cell phone. "I'm going to call for the cops and an ambulance." His voice was clipped and serious. "Then I'll hustle around and get your wife."

"Go away," Mr. Moyen screamed. A rage he couldn't swallow rose in his throat and choked him. His head was full of pounding hammers. He wanted to take one of the hammers and make a dent in Mr. Proctor's skull. "You all need to go away. I'm taking the next trolley. There's an early morning meeting and plenty of work to do."

"Well, hell, fella," he said, patting Mr. Moyen's shoulder and stepping backwards, squinting. "They must've really whacked you one. Stay put and I'll be back in a minute with the little lady."

Mr. Proctor punched three numbers, brought the phone to his ear, and jogged across the rutted tracks toward Mr. Moyen's home.

He turned and shouted. "Everything'll be just fine."

When Mr. Proctor disappeared around the corner of the diner, young Mr. Moyen stood up, swayed in place and trudged eastward along the looping trolley track. There were many avenues yet to travel, any number of serpentine paths. With a grim smile, he staggered toward the beckoning arms of the dark, deceitful dawn.

BABY

While lukewarm water pummels the cavity of a plucked, headless carcass, the giblet bag clings to the ribbed walls, still frozen despite a twenty-minute spin on the microwave platter. Mitchell Ringold turns up the heat and shakes the bird's rubbery legs. He yanks the slab of neck fat, working his hand into the yaw, insinuating his nails beneath the bag. He claws and tugs but manages only to gouge cold chunks. He is left holding a dripping, slimy, gag-all catch—kidney, gizzard, and shredded wrap, a pulpy mass of bloody eviscerate. He raises butcher's hands and thinks, all for love. No wonder in the decades before this latest marriage, he avoided all but the most basic forms of cooking—the oval of frozen meat, the simplicities of toast, the marvel of boiled water.

Leaving the bird beneath the scalding stream, Ringold scrapes the gunk into the disposal, wipes his hands on a dish towel and stabs his fist into the drawer. With the spaghetti fork, he will pry the bag loose before slamming the stuffer in the oven.

In this precarious time, the bird would make dinner and lunch for a good three days. Living on takeout would have been the simplest thing: at least three French restaurants in downtown Greenwich would have been happy to do special favors for such an old customer. But over the last two weeks, in the vagaries that come with the family way, Mina became oddly insistent on home cooking, family-style cooking, like she got at the only restaurant she'd let Ringold take her to. Real Fine Dine was an appalling place within smelling distance of Turnpike Exit 4. Ringold shudders to think of the fat folksy waitress and her surly disposition, those bowls of bleached peas, salty red potatoes, sugary stewed carrots, that greasy platter of crusty black meatloaf. He can't even get a decent glass of wine there. The house wine came from the bottom of a massive jug. It was Merlot, long gone to vinegar and trailing a whiff of gasoline.

"I can't go back," Ringold fumed when they got to the car.

"I loved it," Mina declared. She smiled and settled back, resting her hands just above the pulsing mound. Through her shirt, Ringold saw where Baby was kicking. "It's real home cooking. It's what we've got to get used to. When Baby gets here, we'll be home every night. I'm beyond the point where I'm up to cooking. When you were in the john, the waitress said they do takeout."

"I can't eat that stuff. I'll die."

Mina laughed.

"Well, I'll guess you'll have to die. Because I'm not cooking till Baby's out and I'm feeling better. It makes me sick to look at raw, uncooked things. I want home-style cooking and I'm going to have it. We've talked about the alternative."

"We need to hire a cook."

"No way! I hate having strangers around."

"Well, I'm not going to cook. Not at my age."

"No problem. I have their number. They serve breakfast, lunch, and dinner. They even deliver."

"All right! I'll try. I'll try to cook."

"I want it simple. I can't eat anything fancy."

Ringold, who hated supermarkets but loved Mina, took this belated plunge into domestic cookery. He shopped for food and prepared the meals. He found what it was like to bang carts with the hurried masses, and then what it was like to wash crud from lettuce, boil canned peas, singe roast beef, and slap ground meat into balls. He kept slicing his fingers. Bleeding flesh was one of the costs of loving Mina. His three previous marriages had foundered because he had refused to love his wives. He had always been just who he was—this difficult person, grumpy, imperious, intimidating, a winner all the way, with his niche near the top, a network vice-president of programming at ABC. Over the years, he had ratings and sponsors and producers to worry about. Wives were surely a problem, as were the barking lawyers of wives, but they were best left to his own barking lawyers. It was preferable to stay at the office or in his city apartment, far better to dance bicoastal or shut himself in his study.

But Mina was the first wife who was not an underling, a cringing climber with the mountain of desire of either the cutting cliffs of the entertainment industry or the social pinnacles of Old World Greenwich. With Mina he had done the cringing, the climbing, all the placating, even the compromising. He found himself making most of the promises. He was amazed that she liked but didn't need him. She had her own life, her own career, and her own reconverted farmhouse just northeast of Greenwich. By age thirty-seven Mina Grant had made executive editor of Spectacle Books, trailing a decade-long string of megahits. Finally, after an expensive chase, she accepted him. He then prepared the image of a marriage made for gourmet restaurants, long trips and fast cars, these lovers and advisors peeling along in adjacent lanes, chatting on the cell phone. Shortly before the wedding, he moved in with her. He had gotten rid of his escape routes: he sold his house in New Canaan and his Upper East Side apartment— all rent controlled as it was. Mina wouldn't stand for nights over in the city. It was his job to get home—to their house by law but hers in fact.

Shortly after their honeymoon in Moscow, he listened astonished to her sudden talk of *baby, baby, baby*. This from Mina, who had scoffed at the notion before. Rather than blowing up, stomping his feet, and moving out, as he had when his other wives were crazy enough to talk about *baby*, Ringold listened, and he listened. He found himself saying, "Yes, well yes, I guess so, yes." All the while his stomach roiled, and he felt himself sliding into a pit. *Baby!* Lest he'd seem insufficiently enthusiastic, he found himself hiking his voice to the compliant pitch Mina expected. He controlled one-fourth of network prime time programming, but he didn't control Mina. She had him over this very large barrel. Love had him rolling back and forth, feet off the ground, holding on, looking silly. Love had him saying yes, yes to *baby*, he who had always seen babies as clogs to the body, wallet, and soul, necessary evils for others to produce, an inevitable downside in the creation of adult television viewers.

Now sweating at the sink, feeling slightly like a killer, Ringold jabs the bird with bent prongs. His hand slips and slashes the scalding water. He drops the fork, cuddles his fist, and jumps around. The giblets are still rock solid. He is about to declare an impasse and shove it back in the microwave, but he is arrested by Mina's muffled screams.

He leans forward and slides open the window. Early spring air bites his face. The window seems a TV screen. The scruffy mole-humped lawn and budding trees resemble a placid set, though greatly in need of color and lighting. Again, Mina screams.

"Put it down, Jake! Let 'er go!"

From the left, Jake Barnes, the cat, trots a few feet ahead of the waddling, full-blown Mina, four days overdue, her black hair a streaming tangle, her loose white gown flapping.

"Put it down! You'll kill it. You'll kill the poor thing."

In his jaws, Jake Barnes holds a blue jay, a prize catch. His gait brims with nature's pride, but he keeps looking back, uncertain, his eyes scrunched.

Ringold's heart stabs.

"Stop running! You'll trip in a rut."

With the suddenness of computer spatter on a scrolling screen, facts assail him: a month ago, Baby dropped and then a week ago Baby dropped again. Baby's head is now fully engaged, down deep in the pelvis, upside down and butting the softening, dilating plug. Gravity strains, membranes stretch, and there she is running, chasing that spoiled, ugly cat.

Jake Barnes circles back and swishes beneath Mina's swatting hand and snapping fingers. With the balance of nature tilting against her, she can't waddle and bend at the same time.

Ringold's chest pain switches channels. It's in his stomach now. Acid burns.

"Stop chasing the ratter! It's nature."

"It's gross! He's going to kill it. Jake! Stop! Don't be gross! Stop! Stop!"

With his slightly bubbled paunch shifting inside his cotton sweater, Ringold hustles from the sink, skitters through the breakfast nook, yanks open the back door, slams out the porch screen door, and thumps down four wooden steps. He runs pigeon-toed, gasping. Mina has chased Jake Barnes back to the garage and almost has him cornered. The bird is dead by now, Ringold realizes, scared to death probably—what with the ambush, the crunching feathers, and this massive, wailing woman. It's enough to make Ringold drop dead. Twenty yards away, Jake Barnes crouches and cowers, hunching backwards, dragging his kill, protecting it.

Mina suddenly freezes and arches up. She spreads her legs like the prongs of a large compass and puts her hands to her ears. In a second, she grabs her loins, and spins to face him.

"Oh, Mitch!" she gasps. "It happened. I'm soaked. It's a flood down there. Hurry! Get a towel!"

Ringold stops. "I'll get a white one. In the meantime, don't move!"

Ringold clambers for the house, his heart all hammers, his head bursting, stomach afire. All those books and classes didn't entirely fail him. He knows there's trouble if the water runs brown: he'll have to call emergency and then drive like a maniac, horn blasting, lights flashing. If the fluid is clean, he'll dial the doctor, grab her stuff, and zoom to the hospital.

Ringold doesn't go ten feet before his brain snaps into place. He stops, yanked by a chain, and spins.

"What am I doing?" he spatters. He hustles toward the arrested Mina, her eyes bulging and lips trembling.

"I'm not getting a towel. I don't need a towel. If your gown is discolored, we go right to the car. I'll phone the hospital on the way."

Ringold slides to his knees. Like a child peeking under a tent, he lifts the hem and gathers cloth in bunches, feeling for wetness, bringing it to his face. He rolls up the damp and now soppy linen. Soon he's standing, holding her crumpled gown to the light, exposing massive hams—her hips were so thin—inside those stretch panties. He squeezes fistfuls and the fluid runs in clear rills over his wrists. His heart loosens. He wants to sing, but his bowels go squishy.

"It's okay. It's clear. We're fine, Mina. Baby's fine. Just try to relax and we'll be on our way."

"Ugh! OMIGOD!" Mina hunches over and hugs her womb.

Ringold panics: *she's* having the heart attack! He drops the gown and squeezes his head.

"What is it? What is it?"

Her face strains and her neck pulses. She huffs, puffs— HHHH—HHHH—HHHH—HHHH—now snorting, like a grampus.

"Are you timing it!" she gasps. "HHHH—HHHH— HHHH!"

"Timing what?"

"HHHH—HHH—HHH—HH."

Her breathing subsides and Ringold perceives.

"That's labor? What a dope I am!"

He checks his Rolex, trying to set the automatic timer.

"It must have been 12:14."

"Get the towel, please! I'm still dripping."

"Let's get into the house. Let it drip! I'll call the doctor, but we have to go."

"I want to change."

"You can't change. There's no time to change. I'll get a towel and the stuff and then we go. No messing around!"

Ringold is shocked by his tone. His cowed, compliant veneer had gone the way of Mina's water. He let the beast slip out, the snappish dictatorial beast, all growl and impatience, the chained creature he frequently let loose on incompetent producers or lazy assistants. Repentant, fearing Mina's backlash, Ringold reacquires his kindest tone. "Let me help you, darling."

With his left hand supporting her elbow and his right hand wrapped around her back, he guides her to the house. At the foot of the steps lays the dead blue jay.

Ringold groans, "I just remembered. I was trying to clean out the chicken. I left the water running."

"Go, you idiot!" Mina shoves him. "I can walk."

Ringold kicks the blue jay into the wood chips and stamps up the steps. Barging into the kitchen, he splashes, and skids to the counter. Water pours over the ledge, running down the cabinets and across the tile. Like a canoe adrift, the oven stuffer floats and turns. Ringold shuts the spigot and yanks the stopper. With a suck, the cresting water heaves and subsides. Ringold turns. The water has washed across the tile, down two steps and into the family room. He slides to the far wall and grabs the phone.

"What a mess!" Mina shouts. "You wrecked my house. We can't go anywhere till we clean this up."

"Don't come in here! You'll fall. This floor's like a grease slick."

He jabs the memory button and number four, the doctor's code. He sails across the floor, pulling the long cord. He steadies himself on the doorpost and gives the phone to Mina.

"Forget the floor. We're at least twenty minutes from the hospital. We're not taking any chances with Baby."

"You're right. But we should at least call Martin."

Martin Stavitz is their close friend and neighbor, a recently axed IBM senior executive, settling softly to earth under his golden parachute. In these weeks he is always looking for something to do. For a man used to crunching deals on the international market, there never seems to be enough house for him to putter around in.

"Martin'll help. I'll ring him from the car."

Mina's body lurches. She drops the phone. It splashes.

The receptionist says, "Hello? Hello? Doctor's office."

Ringold looks at his watch.

"Only four minutes! What's Baby doing? The first one's supposed to take forever."

Mina is huffing, puffing. She's draped over the counter.

The receptionist continues. "Are you there? Is this an emergency?"

Ringold gathers the phone from the floor.

"This is Mitchell Ringold, Mina Grant's husband. Tell Cronin to get his ass to the hospital! Mina's water broke and she's having contractions four minutes apart."

He slams the dripping phone back on the wall.

Mina is beginning to straighten. "That one tore me up."

"Sit down and rest! I'll get the stuff."

Ringold skids across the tile and into the hallway. The water has run almost to the stairs and might not stop until it soaks into the living room carpet.

"Mitch," Mina yells. "Don't forget a towel. I'm still dripping."

Ringold's Porsche is not family friendly. He lowers Mina into her seat, a white towel stuffed between her legs. He positions her feet in the dark space beneath the dash. Soon, he races down the humped and twisty roads, punching numbers on the car phone, making declarations and requests, all the while negotiating L-turns and sliding through stop signs, his yellow flashers clicking. On the road to the hospital, stark brown trees stir at the tips with green buds. Purple water stands in patches. Gray mottled clouds bulge and tumble. Spring quickens. After one fierce contraction, Mina lies back. Her head settles beneath the sloping rear window; a bulky feather pillow bolsters her lower back. One hand settles on his thigh and the other grips the armrest. As the next contraction surges, her fingers wrench his pants and nails dig into his flesh.

"Breathe," he whispers, now remembering his lessons, peering forward to get a jump on the curve, his own stomach tumbling as a pickup truck's left front tire sneaks over the center line. Ringold jerks the wheel to the right.

"Dumb bastard! Fool!" Mina moans. "Watch what you're doing! You should've taken the Volvo."

Their new family wagon. Ringold hates driving it.

"Breathe through the pain. Put your mind elsewhere. Watch a lily pad floating on a pond."

"This car is a rotten tin can!" Mina gasps, clawing close to his groin.

"I would've taken the Volvo, darling, but we're in a hurry. This car is made for these roads."

"You're a dumb beer-brained bastard!"

"Just breathe," Ringold mildly replies. And smiles. The book was right. Scapegoat therapy. Vicious. Harmless. Her hand relaxes.

"Whew! That was a bad one." Ringold glances. She settles farther back, face pale, eyes closed, lips fused, awaiting the next squeeze. "*Are* you my darling?"

"Yes, I am. Of course. Totally. We're twelve minutes out. We're doing fine. They'll be waiting for us. Try to relax."

Ringold slows at the red light, looks both ways, and blows through. His mind settles into comfortable lanes. With these definite miles ahead, he has this particular thing to do. His mind drifts not far from the floating lily pad. How would this play on the little screen? Your basic ninety-minute movie of the week. A world premiere. *Middle Age Madness.* A fifty-one-year-old lawyer and a thirty-eight-year-old something. Now what would the female lead be? An executive whatever, a cutthroat careerist. He'd figure it out later. In the first scene, Bart Gunther finds out and is totally surprised. With golf clubs clattering, he's on the way out the door. Amanda ambushes him with the news. The man would be good looking, without Ringold's chunky lumpishness, his thinning gray hair, and his fat, hairy legs. Somebody like Richard Gere, but less expensive. It would be the writer's problem to make morning sickness a hip New Age thing, flip and funny, not like the real McCoy, those awful months of Mina gagging and puking, the terrible tub by the bed. Whenever she missed, Ringold got down on all fours, holding his breath, sopping it up. With Mina prostrate, Ringold had stayed home. For three straight weeks. With the magic of fax, e-mail, and conference calls, he'd had no trouble running his office. He could lay on the pressure almost as well from afar as he could up close and personal. An acidic memo was about as useful as an ambiguous smile. He was even able to help Mina with some of her backlog. He knew her taste, so with her permission, he pruned the unsolicited submissions. With his absolute contempt for agents and his qualified disdain for writers, he applied his script-reading shorthand: you had five minutes to bury the hook. What she might like, he set aside. The slush he piled in the corner for Mina's assistant to cart away. But none of this would do for his Movie-of-the-Week. Instead, there'd be the baby shower with all her feminist friends. Two or three identity crises. All the trouble with decorating Baby's room. A *Money Pit* kind of thing. They wouldn't do the frozen oven stuffer. Too obstetric. Jake Barnes's dead bird would have to go. Too sinister. The water would break, and they'd do a madcap chase. The cop car in the rear view. Twists and turns. Plenty of near wrecks. Low comedy. Everything but a runaway piano passing the car. The roadblock and explanations. Bart Gunther has connections. He's friends with all the cops. We see the police escort and then straight cut to a commercial.

Mina moans. He looks at the clock. Three minutes out. Ringold's chest tightens, but it loosens when he spies the turnpike ramp. In the fast lane, he will open it up and reach the hospital exit in five minutes. Mina's hand relaxes as Ringold tops eighty-five. The closer he gets, the more his nerves twist. He feels the stab of old worries, none of them easily filmable. Will he be able to take the sleepless nights, the dirty diapers? Ringold tends to despise other people's children—they never behave, always whining in restaurants or acting up on airplanes—and the parents are boring and ludicrous, taking pride in absurd things. All that jabber about formula or breastfeeding, cloth or disposable diapers, pediatricians and ear infections, gifted children and accelerated learning. Already, Mina is a breast-feeding snob who hates daycare centers and disposable diapers. Ringold pictures himself kneeling in front of the toilet, shaking baby poop from the folds and wringing brown water. Already, Mina is certain she will be a stay-at-home professional mother—writing her rejection letters and editing her manuscripts between the naps, the crying, and the baths. Mina has vowed never to go anywhere. And what will Ringold have to do? Already, he feels jealous: he doesn't want to get left out, but he can't imagine retiring. How will it be to leave the house in the morning or bounce between coasts? Will he do day trips to L.A.? Where will it take them all? He's been doing arithmetic. When he is sixty-one, Baby will be ten; when he's seventy-three, Baby will be twenty-two. Not to forget the fact that men his age—and older—drop dead all the time.

He pulls into the lot and Mina is gasping. She's down to two minutes, barely recovering in time for the next spasm.

Leaving the car on the curb at the emergency room entrance, Ringold helps Mina to the door. They are met with a wheelchair. Mina is whisked away, and Ringold is pointed to a reception area. There's a line, seven people long. His heart stabs. He fears he'll be late for the show. In a kind of fit, he reaches into his wallet and digs out his coverage card.

He bustles to the front of the line and sticks his head inside the window. The receptionist is on the phone, ignoring him. Behind him, someone is shouting. He tosses his card on a pile of papers and backs off. The receptionist looks up, startled, irritated.

"We're pre-registered. The card'll tell you who we are. Do whatever you do. I'll sign whatever I have to later."

Ringold runs, slow, then faster. *This will make a good scene.* He toggles off the switch and fixes attention on the crowded corridor—the wheelchairs, the doctors, the parked gurneys. He weaves and dodges, his heart thumping, his veins filled with air, his breathing clogged, his head light. The perfect place for a heart attack.

At the far end of a corridor, maybe fifty yards down, he sees Mina being hurried through another door. Now he dodges a moving gurney. It carries a man his age. He looks dead, pasty, and gray. Ringold bounces off a wall and picks up his stride. He doesn't want to miss a thing. She's probably less than two minutes or maybe even ready to push. He races, races, doing everything he can to catch up to Mina and Baby.

Mina breathes with raspy regularity, her hands clutching the sidebars of the birthing bed, her gown pulled just below her breasts, exposing her rounded stomach and scribbled stretch marks. Mina's navel, once an imploded plug of dimpled folds, is now a medallion of red brazed streaks, a cabalistic coin glazed with a runic skein. With indifferent abandon, her legs are cast apart. The birthing room lights are soft amber. Ringold stands to the side, patting her head, mumbling words. He is shaken, appalled to see a brown watery stream gush from beneath her. It is followed by bursts of farting squirts. Nurse Mollars, her gray hair cropped, smiles and gathers the sheet, wiping Mina clean.

"Just rest, dear," she coos. "You're doing great."

Mina seems not to hear. Her energy has gone all the way

inside. She's garnering strength, entering those places where women have always given birth—in high corn fields, next to swollen rivers, in steaming jungles, fetid cargo holds, and murky huts, in small cars, clean condominiums, bustling train stations, and contagious hospitals.

The nurse has a vinyl glove on her right hand. With her eyes looking away, she examines Mina. Her shoulder dips; she leans forward. The lines on her forehead wriggle.

"Good!" she exclaims. "You're there. Ready to push. Dr. Cronin is just down the hall. It'll take a few minutes to break down the bed and set up the cart."

She yanks back the curtain door.

"Mary, tell Dr. Cronin Mina is ready."

The bed grows stirrups that stick way out. Mina's feet find the straps. The bottom of the bed pulls away. She's hanging near the edge.

The room bursts into commotion. Mary, all smiling pudge and brisk motion, flicks through the curtain and smacks the switch. The ceiling screams with light: the dim cavern has become a florescent hollow. Ringold examines the sparkling faucets and the standing circular mirror. Mary wheels a cart laden with hardware: there are seventeen different kinds of hot dog tongs, a multitude of scalpels, scissors, and pincers. A small hammer. A host of hypodermic syringes and packets of needles. Three bulb aspirators. A pile of gauze, a reel of fish line. Dr. Cronin, who Ringold never much liked, bounces in, his smiling joking self. He's all gowned-up, projecting the upbeat manner of a game show host.

"Hey, Mitch," he calls. "How're the ratings?"

Cronin hustles to the sink, turns the taps, and scrubs.

Ringold rubs Mina's quavering hand and strokes her cheek, her chin, her forehead. He ignores the question. "How's she doing?"

Cronin turns back with dripping hands upraised. "Perfect," he blurts.

Nurse Mollars applies the towel and snaps surgical gloves over and down. She turns off the spigot.

"Her labor was incredibly quick. I was playing tennis in Ridgefield. I had to fly to make it. She's doing great. She's made for babies. She can easily have three more. It's been a real breeze."

Ringold wants to disagree. It tears his stomach to see her poised and ready to writhe, her face smeared with sweat.

"You're doing great, darling." He dabs her cheek.

"We're ready," Cronin says. He wheels a circular stool to Mina's open legs. He isn't smiling. He squats on his seat and with an index finger rubs the rim of her vagina, tugging and stretching, making faster and faster ovals.

"It's all up to you, Mina," Cronin says. "It's time to push. When I say go, I want you to bear down and push. Ready! Now push!"

Ringold's chest seizes; his throat strangles. The doctor and nurses are yelling, calling. Mina strains and grunts, her face, usually so pale, is tomato red, swollen, contorted, her veins bulging. Ringold wants to call the whole thing off. Cancel the show. Mina stops and sags. With his finger, Cronin tugs the oval. Her vulva seems a pulpy fruit, peach red, turning inside out. Cronin squints into the tunnel.

"That was tremendous. The head's right there. See this, Mitch." Cronin pulls back a flap and touches a swirl of gray goo. "This is the head. With a little push, the head will crown. Mina, dear, just give me a little push."

Mina breathes deeply and strains. Again, the doctor and nurses yell. This time Ringold joins the melee, this poltergeist spew of words.

"Let it burn! Push! Push through the burn! Come on!"

The gray goo becomes a bubbled mass.

"Hold it there," Cronin says. "The baby will be out in no time."

Mina lifts her head and looks in the mirror.

"I see Baby. I don't believe it."

"You're doing great," Ringold mumbles, his mind a-twirl with all those worries about birth defects. Two heads. No arms. And then the movie where the monster tears right out of mother's belly.

Just beneath Baby's head, Cronin slips in a needle and injects a clear stream. He waits ten seconds and then snips three times. He puts the scissors on the tray and lifts the aspirator.

"One little push and we have the head. The worst is over. Now we get to the good part."

The grayish bubble inflates into a ball and soon Ringold sees a velvety ear smudged with white. With three quick squeezes, Cronin extracts fluid from the mouth and nose. The head turns. A bluish face with puffy lips rises from the earth like a balloon.

Mina gasps and sits halfway up. She points to the mirror.

"Baby!" She grabs Ringold's hand. "I see my baby."

Ringold's mouth works without words. He's a boob tube without sound.

"Push a little bit!" The doctor cups two fingers under the neck and gently delivers the top shoulder and then the lower one. In seconds, the blue mottled chest and waist emerge and then with two-handed motion, Cronin pulls out the newborn.

Nurse Mollars yells, "He's beautiful!"

Cronin snickers. "Look again, Jane! You're blind."

Ringold sees why. It moves away from him, the cord dangling. Cronin holds her up, eyes closed, hands grasping, the little mouth pursing After she wails, Cronin places her on Mina's chest. Ringold watches the color change to a blotched pink.

"Oh, my God!" Mina laughs. "She's peeing all over me." She brings the baby's lips to her left breast.

The cord, now clamped, slowly ceases to pulse. Ringold rubs Mina's face and then with a shaky finger, he touches Baby's wet papery cheek. Cronin offers him a pair of scissors.

"Take it, Mitch! It's time a guy your age does something worthwhile. Cut it there! Right there."

With his left hand steadying his right wrist Ringold snips it—quick and clean—and sets his daughter free.

"Everyone'll be so excited," Mina proclaims. Her hand turns the tap. Inside the hanging hospital gown, wide open at the back, she stands barefoot on the bathroom tile. Behind the curtain, the shower gushes. "Mom and Dad'll want to fly right in. After I get cleaned up, we'll make all our calls."

Mina's the one with the extended family. Her parents are still very much alive, having last year left West Allis, Wisconsin, for an active retirement in Treasure Island, Florida. Her three brothers and four sisters are scattered about the more desirable Milwaukee suburbs—Wawatosa, Brookfield, Glenside, Fox Point. Ringold has only two calls to make right away, one to his mildly estranged brother, Marv, a psychiatrist in San Diego, the other to his octogenarian uncle in Orlando, his father's brother, Jack, a Disney World buff, a lonely widower without children, the last of only two Mohegans. Ringold's late mother, whom he doesn't remember, was an only child.

"I don't know why it is," Mina wonders, stepping out of her gown and into the cubicle, "but having a baby is like coming home. My parents will finally think of me as a success."

"They've always thought of you as a success."

"How would you know?" she laughs.

"I'll let you get your shower. You'll feel better."

"I feel great. Like I could lift a car. I was right not to let them give me that pain killer. It only hurts when I sit. I'm never going to sit down again. What are you going to do?"

"Go down to the nursery and watch them clean up Baby."

"It's Marsha now."

Already Ringold misses Marsha. Five minutes ago, when the nurse wheeled her away, his stomach swooned and ached. Ringold does not want her out of his sight. Last spring, they ran a docudrama about infant abductions, a true-life tale, dramatically reenacted with only a few enhancements. Ringold still sees the maniac woman dressed as a nurse sneaking the baby down a back stairwell.

"I also want to check security measures."

"Just don't be abusive!"

"I won't be abusive, darling. I'll only ask questions."

Ringold hustles down the hall. He all but runs to the glass wall and stares at the cribs. There are ten babies—six white, three black, one Asian—all sleeping on their backs in diapers and T-shirts. Ringold tastes fear: he doesn't see her. He wants to tap the glass—no, bang with both fists—till he finds another bank of windows. He hustles over and sees her just on the other side, attended by a large nurse, who wipes tar-like excrement from her little behind. While Marsha squalls and kicks and seems all rage, the nurse calmly dabs, glancing up to smile.

"She's mine," Ringold smiles, tapping the glass and poking his chest.

The nurse nods and makes elaborate mouth motions. "Seven pounds." Seven fingers. "Three ounces." Three fingers. "Twenty-two inches." Two then more two fingers.

Ringold watches the nurse fasten a diaper and slip Marsha's arm into a T-shirt. Footsteps skid behind him. He turns and sees a frazzled young man, maybe twenty-one, carrying a little boy, maybe three. The man pulls next to Ringold and looks down.

"There's your sister. Jimmy, say 'hi' to Chrissy."

Ringold doubts himself. In a panic, he scrunches his eyes and sees her face, a rising balloon, and those puffy lips. Mine. The man keeps talking. He's tapping the glass.

"Hey there, Chrissy. Say 'hi' to Jimmy, your big brother." He reaches with Jimmy's hand and rubs the glass. "Say 'hi' and 'bye-bye.' We'll come back later. We have to go see Mommy."

Ringold's heart twists with consternation. He feels like

grabbing the guy by the shirt and straightening him out. But then he pulls himself together. It's one mistake that will do no harm, another illusion playing on the magic glass. It'll be something to tell, a story for Mina, and now that he thinks of it, an ending to his television movie, though this time it will be Bart Gunther who gets his own baby wrong. They'll play it to the max—the new father coo-cooing, tapping the glass, making faces, jumping up and down, the baby impervious, staring straight at him, seeing a moving blur. They'll even give the blur from the baby's perspective, and then they'll see the mother, coming up from behind, pushing the bassinet, smiling, laughing, and watching her husband whooping in the hallway, going wild over the wrong baby. The audience will love it. They won't want it to end. Even when the credits roll, they won't want it to end. There will be Ringold in the semblance of Richard Gere, still jumping, his arms flapping, with people passing and staring and Mina right behind him, waiting to break the news.

ANCHORITE

Wakefield follows the large man up the creaking back stairs toward the attic flat, which, from the street, seemed a squashed top hat tilting from a wobbly head. From the second story apartment bursts the boisterous glee of *Sesame Street*, but the words are strangled by two sobbing children. They hike their voices to a level just below the hateful bellow and bleat of mutual spouse abuse.

Fallow turns the corner and nods toward the door.

"Don't let 'em scare you off. Once in a blue moon, they get into a tiff. What's a marriage without a few fights?"

Wakefield hears, *Shut up, you bitch!* and *Take your hands off me!* To the sound of breaking glass, he sighs and trails Fallow into the narrow stairwell.

The smack of hand on flesh cleaves the air. *So, you wanna get tough? We'll get tough!* is followed by *Put down the knife, you pig!*

"Pretty soon," Fallow declares, "he'll bang the hell out of there and find a bottle to crawl into."

Grasping both rails, the landlord heaves his winded bulk to the next step. Wakefield follows, his face not three inches from Fallow's undulating hams.

Furniture turns over. Wakefield winces and his stomach swims. If he was the man he'd been that morning, he'd be inside the apartment, straightening the guy out. He'd do what it took to save the children. At sixty, Wakefield could still throw most men across a room. But it's already too late. He failed, absolutely. Downstairs, a door slams.

"There goes Chucky. About midnight, he'll come back all drunk and sorry. Then they'll make up. She moans and he grunts. Their bedroom's right on top of mine."

With his last bit of oomph, Wakefield rattles Fallow's cage.

"On the phone, you said it was quiet."

Living atop the horror seems a proper kind of punishment.

"Most of the time it is, but for two hundred a month, you can't expect the Waldorf Astoria."

At the top of the steps, Fallow wheezes, fumbles with a key and clicks open the door.

Two musty rooms are carved beneath a steeply pitched roof. Two dormers offer constricted access to the mottled sky and bare shivery limbs. To fling himself into space, Wakefield will first have to crawl to the window on his knees, belly down, appropriately. A bit of a squeeze, but he'll fit.

"I'll take it for a week. I need that long to figure out what I'm doing."

Fallow laughs. "In my book, a week's the same as a month. I want the first and last month's rent and one month's security. That's six hundred. Up-front."

Wakefield reminds himself he's still nobody's fool.

"I'll give you fifty. After a week, if I'm still here, we can settle up proper. This place isn't even up to code."

Wakefield pulls out a wad. He peels two twenties and slips out a ten. He waves the bills like a hankie.

"No way!"

"Cash. Right now. Take it or leave it. There are better door-steps than this. A motel would be just as good."

It wouldn't: he'd be too easy to find.

He rustles the money. Fallow's eyes follow the green.

"Okay. A week." Fallow squints and holds out his hand. "Then we settle up."

"We'll see," Wakefield sighs. "I may be long gone."

Fallow pockets his loot.

"What'd you say your name was?"

"Smith. Joe Smith."

A thirteen-inch TV set burns on the chilled rutted planks. Beneath the bare screaming bulb, Wakefield shifts in the squeaky aluminum lawn recliner, his hands tucked beneath his thighs, his thick fingers picking the frayed nylon edges of saggy blue and white webbing. After deciding to leave his life, he took the chair from the shed and the black and white TV from the attic. With an exploding heart, he happened to spy his daughter's old sleeping bag. While he didn't wish to live, he also didn't want to freeze. Later, upon first rolling it out, he found it mildewed. As he twisted in insomniac contortions, he relished the misery. A proper penance: to lie awake, tortured, in the clasp of a raunchy dump. Like doing the afterlife in a leaky coffin.

While waiting for the end—by whatever means, spectacular or mundane, isn't yet clear—Wakefield remains paralyzed before the tube, his spirit alternately drifting in dolor or razed by guilt. His hunger, once a jabbing blade spindling his guts, now after five days merely aches and stings like an infected laceration. The TV drone seems a watchful turnkey. Wakefield never shuts it off, never changes the channel. Even while enduring masochistic visions—he sees the shocked, angry, and grieving multitude moving past the lovely head propped so primly on embroidered satin—Wakefield never shuts it off, never changes the channel. It burns through afternoon forays with *The Bold and the Beautiful, General Hospital* and *Dr. Phil* and night owl replays of *Entertainment Tonight, Forensic Files* and *Rush Limbaugh*, a cavalcade of hand-wringing dilemmas, medical conundrums, reenacted disasters, sex perverts, Hollywood minutes, and right-wing diatribes. It all plays as Muzak to Wakefield's throbbing woe. Even as Kelly Ripa and her changing cast of friends affect the comforting banality of well-adjusted, socially progressive, cheerfully enlightened adults, Wakefield remains within the terrible bubble. In the afternoons, he barely distinguishes between screaming recriminations on *The Bold and the Beautiful* and the serial warfare running below. Only when the police siren approaches, does Wakefield stir his weakened body and turn down the sound. The siren gets closer and closer. The cruiser blares to a stop at the curb. He sees the twirling blue lights, hears the banging at the front door, Fallow's guttural shouts, the tramping of feet on the stairs. Wakefield gets ready to make one move or the other—either to answer the door or leap through the open window. But the feet stop too soon. More screams rise. They force open the door. When Chucky is dumb enough to resist arrest, Wakefield turns the sound back up and collapses into his seat.

On the sixth and penultimate day, a Sunday, Wakefield's panicked wife shows up at the door. On the screen, the game is in sudden death overtime and the Dolphins are lining up to kick a field goal. The Bengals call time.

"Open up, Bill. If you're alive let me in. You owe it to me. Bill. It's been thirty-four years. You need to come home. If you don't answer, the police will come up. They're downstairs. I don't want to find your body."

It's time to jump. With the cops out there, she won't be the first to see the body. As quietly as possible, he rises from the chair. In his weakness, he leans on the arm and the thing tilts sideways. He lands face down amid a jumbled clatter.

Mary weeps a sob of joyful, enraged grief.

"Thank God! You idiot! Open up! Open up now! You've done enough to us. You've done enough. We're sick of having you dead. It's time to come back. I love you. Audrey loves you. Everything'll be fine."

Wakefield stays down and crawls toward the open window.

"Say something, damn it!" Her shoulder pounds the door. The walls rattle.

Wakefield gets to the sill and settles on his haunches. Down headfirst. Like Marie. But he supposes Mary deserves a last word.

"I can't go back. I'm a killer. I can't face Audrey or anybody. I was on watch. I let it happen. You don't understand. You're not a killer."

He'd lifted his eyes from the newspaper. His two-year-old granddaughter was giggling and waving from the outside edge of the balcony. Before he could budge, she removed her other hand to clap and landed headfirst on the hardwood floor.

With the baby convulsing on his lap, Wakefield sped to the hospital. Her skull was fractured, her brain swollen. They told him she'd need a miracle to make it. If he signed the consent forms, they'd try surgery. After they wheeled her away, he couldn't stand being stuck inside his skin. He made his choice. Before going, he left a message on their voice mail.

"You idiot! You left too soon. Marie's alive."

"She's a vegetable."

"She's not. They were able to control the intracranial swelling. She's conscious and knows us. She's going home next week. There doesn't seem to be any permanent damage."

On TV, the football sails through the uprights. The Dolphins win and the Bengals lose.

Wakefield feels the air going out of him.

"Bill! Are you there?"

Standing up, he cracks his head on the slanted ceiling and slumps to all fours.

"I was giving myself a week to get up the guts to leave. I was too weak to get it done."

"There's nothing to get done. There's nothing to do but come home. Open the door, damn you!"

"How do I know you're not lying?"

"Bill! I've had enough. I'm telling the truth. Everybody thinks you're a fool."

Wakefield's head wobbles. Almost a week without food. Some water. He closes the shuddering window. He shouts over the noise. "Stop kicking the door. How'd you find me?"

He was in Easton, a good fifty miles from Baltimore.

"I hired a detective. You pulled some money from a MAC machine seventeen miles from here. For an idiot trying to hide, it was a dumb mistake. Yesterday, the detective found your car in the Wal-Mart shopping center and called me. I came down last night. The break came while we were canvassing the area. We went to a bar around the corner and happened to show that awful landlord your picture. The Fallow man said you owe him a hundred and fifty bucks. For a hundred and fifty bucks, he'd tell us where to find you. I gave him the money, called the cops, and rushed over here. Now open up! It's over."

THE CRITICAL LIST

While the right side of the car dipped into the yawning earth, my mind swooshed like a deflating tire. On the wheel, my hands went white-knuckle tight. I fought the gravitational suck of unwanted sleep. Blinking my eyes, steadying my wobbly head, I aimed the car into a Western Avenue parking space. It was like guiding a cantankerous elephant from behind.

Directly ahead, pasted high on the hill, like a billboard advertising a better world, the Hollywood sign sparkled in January's late low light.

My first thought was, *aftershock*.

I remembered how it felt when a big one had hit Northridge, flattening apartments, blowing up gas lines, fracturing water mains. Beautiful homes teetered and crumpled. Thirty miles from the epicenter, the studio caught fire and flooded. At home, I lost most of my glasses and plates. For days, off and on, the ground grumbled; bedrock slabs sidled into tenuous repose. Out here, you try to be braced for anything—torrential rains, wildfires, race riots, psycho stranglers. But even "old hands" are never quite braced for shuddering pavements and quavering walls.

Through the windshield, not a single panicked face turned skyward. The humdrum pedestrian muddle was broken only by an ecstatic Rollerblader. Mother Earth was staying put.

Next, I figured my wheel had come off. With my forehead beading and my palms clammy cold, I pushed out and felt my way around the hood. Each step was precarious, wooden, like my sister Loni's ten-month-old son. During my holiday visit east, Thomas had pawed his way along the couch and tumbled between chairs. I staggered back from the fender and expected to see the tire tilting from the axle. But it was right in place, bolted and dirty. Behind the car, up the street, there was no crater. Western Avenue was merely a skein of webby cracks.

I flopped into the driver's seat and wiped my forehead with my sleeve. There was something wrong with me. I had almost passed out. Shadowy faces leaned close, these silent killers—aneurysm, embolism, heart failure, stroke. In the dark lurked row on row of diseases and syndromes I knew nothing about.

In forty-five minutes, I was supposed to meet Delilah Faye at The Blasted Tomato. She was a fairly new actress on *Dawn Becomes the Darkness*, the popular soap I'm head writer for. Delilah plays Tiffany Morganchild, an anorexic, suicidal, lesbian lawyer, who is defending Dawn Desiree, the star of the show. By day, Dawn is a successful Beverly Hills interior decorator. By night, she runs an escort service to the stars. Dawn is currently under indictment for attempted sexual mutilation, malicious mischief, and conspiracy. One of her girls had been beaten by a TV news anchor who resembles Brian Williams. Dawn invited him to her office to discuss a damage settlement. She got him comfortable and then, while screaming rape, tried to castrate him.

By now, I was feeling closer to normal. The sweating had stopped, and I only felt a little shaky. I wanted my day simply to resume—a few drinks, some laughs, and maybe dinner, then home alone. It wasn't much, but what can you ask of Wednesday? Besides, for some months now, I had been laying off the mayhem. I was getting to the age—forty-seven—when I looked forward to putting my pajamas on and reading myself to sleep. I was working through Charles Dickens' *Our Mutual Friend* and had left off where Mr. Boffin inexplicably turns nasty. It occurred to me, though, that I might actually be sick—I never got sick—and, even worse, I might drop dead. People did that. Suddenly. Even in-shape people like me.

I checked the mirror, set the gear, and pulled away. With

hands gripping the wheel, I headed to the emergency room of UCLA Medical Center.

I leaned forward and put my face through the sliding plastic window.

"I felt the world swoon and I started sweating. All over," I said.

"Again, sir, I can't admit you till I get your information."

The pudgy forty-something black woman was copying my insurance card. When she was done, she shooed me away.

"Please have a seat. Someone will be out for you."

Across the room, an old man with a gray face and sparse white hair stared at the clock. A young woman pushed a stroller back and forth with her foot.

A wheelchair barged through double doors. It was pushed by a large black orderly with shaven head and green surgical fatigues. Ms. Harrison pointed at me. I waved off assistance and sat down. We whizzed through double doors and down a long linoleum corridor. It opened into a room with a row of curtained cubicles. We stopped. He pulled open a corner. A gurney was inside.

"Take off your clothes and put that on."

He pointed to a white gown with gray stripes. Behind me, rings rattled as the curtain closed.

With backside fully exposed, I climbed up, knees first, and swung my bum onto a crackling paper sheet. A nurse took my temperature and blood pressure. A technician extracted four vials of blood. Ten minutes later, Michael Collier, a physician's assistant, listened to my story and examined me. He scoped my chest and back, tapped my knees with a hammer, and flashed a light into my eyes. He made me count his fingers. He said nothing and left, brusquely, snubbing me like a real doctor.

A half hour passed with nothing but emergency room sounds—codes and names crackling on the intercom; wheezing from a distant cubicle; the wailing of a boy with a gashed head; a woman puking and calling to God. It occurred to me I was in a low-level triage area, as close to the hospital siding as you can get.

I was already forty minutes late meeting Delilah Faye. I didn't have her number in my phone, but she used the same service as one of my ex-wives. I called and left a message that I was in the emergency room. I also needed to find a bathroom, but I didn't want to miss someone important. I was expecting to see a neurologist or at least a real doctor. I poked my head out. Way up the corridor, nurses were hurrying in and out of a room. To my left, at the end of the curtains, I saw an alcove with vending machines and rest rooms. I scampered on tiptoe, as though I were sneaking across somebody's lawn at midnight. Right after I got back on the gurney, Collier yanked the curtain.

"Just checking to make sure you're still alive."

When I didn't laugh, he said, "Just kidding."

"What's wrong with me?"

"The tests haven't come back from the lab."

"Do you think I have a brain tumor?"

Collier laughed. "I think you have two. One for each hemisphere."

"What!"

"Just kidding. Frankly, I don't think you have anything."

"I have to have something. I almost blacked out."

"I'll see you when the tests come back."

For an hour, I heard hospital noises, and then he returned.

"You can go," he said.

"What do you mean, go?"

"You're okay. You're one of the healthiest people I've seen in months."

"That's not saying much. People come in here and die."

"Some get patched up and we turn them loose. We also get hypochondriacs all the time. They're usually pretty healthy."

"You think I'm a hypochondriac?"

"No, I think you had a near syncope."

"What's that?"

"You almost fainted."

"I know that, but why?"

"Probably your blood pressure dropped. It can happen to anybody. Maybe you didn't eat breakfast and you've been going all day on an empty stomach."

"I had breakfast and lunch."

"Maybe you've been under a lot of stress."

"I've been feeling better than I usually do."

"Any of the big three lately—death, divorce, unemployment?"

"Actually, well, two out of three."

"Which ones and how recently."

"Late last October, my divorce went through."

"Was it rough?"

"Actually, it was the easiest one. My third."

"Geez! What else?"

"Both my parents have died within the year. In March, my mother died of lymphoma. Two weeks after that, my father had a heart valve shut on him. It turned into cardiac arrest and they put him on a respirator. His kidneys went. He got ARDS. He basically conked out."

"The two deaths could do it."

"To tell you the truth, I feel almost as close to them now as I ever did. I believe in ghosts—spirits—whatever you want to call them. I think we're crowded by the dead."

He was frowning, his forehead all wrinkled. "What do you do for a living?"

"I'm a writer."

His forehead bunched some more. "What do you write?"

"I write for *Dawn Becomes the Darkness*, the soap."

He brightened. "When I work nights, I watch that show. My wife loves it, too. It must be interesting work."

"It can be a great release—foisting imaginary disasters on

imaginary people." I made sure we gave rich celebrities the problems of ordinary people—substance abuse, percolating despair, chronic confusion, never enough love. Over and over, we dramatized how having a lot of money only gave people more ways of making themselves miserable. As far as daytime TV went, it was a winning formula. "The bottom line is, I felt fine. There was no reason to faint. It just suddenly happened."

"Did you get inside a hot car? That'll do it sometimes."

"I'd been driving for thirty minutes. Maybe it was the smog. I had my windows open."

He laughed. "What can I say? You have no symptoms. If you get some symptoms, call your doctor."

"Something happened."

"Well, it's not happening now. Sign here." He offered the clipboard. "You can put your clothes on and leave. I need to get back. You know, it's funny. Ever since the last wildfires, there have been fewer accidents but more shootings. How do you figure?"

"Where do I sign?"

I was three hours late and Hollywood reminded me of a cemetery. Those pavement squares of autographed hand-prints made the vestibule of Mann's Chinese Theater seem a mortuary. On the Walk of Fame were more funereal slabs—obituaries inscribed in concrete—scuffed with shoes, splotched with bird lime. All the dead stars, these black holes: Judy and Duke and Betty and Tyrone. A few blocks away, in the Roosevelt Hotel, more than four decades ago, Janis Joplin took an overdose and died.

I turned off Hollywood Boulevard and plunged into The Blasted Tomato. Happy Hour had expired. The smoky de-lu-minated lounge was a sunken scatter of driftwood booths and castaway tables. Along the far wall, an ornately carved, darkly stained facade encased the beveled mirror, ranked shelves, and sparkling bottles. A mob huddled around the long bar and high-back chairs.

I didn't think Delilah would be there, but I gave the place a spin. I sauntered among tables, peering into noisy groups, sizing up couples, and sweeping past lone rangers.

After climbing the lounge's steps, I went to the bar's far end. From under a gargoyle, I had a full view of the crowd. I saw a few faces I knew—some technical guys from the studio, a booking agent who once represented Pia Zadora, a lawyer who made a fortune getting DWI offenders off the hook. A former girlfriend and I spotted each other at the same time. Sondra Slade did the weekend weather for KOKU-TV. Her sudden smile was an open wound, jagged and pulsing. I waved. From under her puffy bleached bouffant, she stuck out her tongue. She pulled some guy's necktie. His jerking head obstructed the line of fire. On a normal day, this would have been amusing, but it wasn't a normal day. I was waiting for the room to fall away and me to tumble into a black hole.

I skirted the sunken lounge, nudging my way through the boozers. A hand clamped my shoulder. I turned. Nate Newell was reaching across a talking couple. A bearded man was analyzing Spielberg and dinosaurs and the woman was nodding her head, eyes glazed over.

"David! Long time, no see."

I had seen Nate just last Friday, but he seemed not to remember. He had been drunk and ranting against the Pulitzer Prize committee. For the third time, he had gotten passed over. Nate was poet-in-residence at USC and supposedly gifted, though I couldn't tell. To me, his poems read like poor prose slashed into arbitrary lines. Five years ago, I met him while taking part in a USC symposium on "Daytime Television and Psychosis." One angry older student in army fatigues, kinky black hair, and ratty pubic beard shook his finger and accused me of exploiting human misery for profit. I replied seriously, ranking myself with physicians, lawyers, and morticians, but the crowd laughed, as though I were joking. The student was hooted down, as moral voices often are. Since then, Nate and I have become pretty good friends.

"Where you sitting?" I yelled, pulling away.

"Back there in the corner. Let me buy you one."

"I'll be right back. I stood somebody up. I need to call and explain."

I was drifting away, waving, and he was smiling. He wasn't drunk. He was happy to see me.

"I was in the emergency room for three hours."

My instinct for the straight cut left him nattering.

"What happened? Nothing's wrong, is it?"

He'd have to wait through the commercials.

"I'll be back in two minutes."

To get some quiet, I headed down the corridor toward the rest rooms. Above where the pay phone used to be hung an erasable graffiti board with its display of slogans, allegations, solicitations, and graphics. I found that Moby Dick is a social disease, that Debbie does do Debbie, that I should call Cockrobin (GSWM) for risky sex, and that poorly drawn penises still resemble misshapen balloons.

I took out my phone and jabbed redial.

Once again, I got Delilah's service. The receptionist's voice was young and scratchy, with a lazy Valley Girl inflection.

"This is David Higginson calling back for Delilah Faye. Has she picked up my message? I'm the emergency room guy."

"She called a little while ago. She said you stood her up."

"I would've called her, but I don't have her number in my phone. I only had the service. It was either stand her up or maybe drop dead. Was she mad?"

"When I said you were in the emergency room, she was *very* relieved. Nothing personal, I'm sure. But it's an ego thing. Being stood up's okay if there's a reason. Say, how *are* you?"

"I had a near syncope."

"Omigod! Really? What's that?"

"I almost fainted, but they don't know why."

"Look, I gotta split. Another line's lighting up. You got a message for Ms. Faye? I'd give you her direct number, but I'm not allowed."

"Tell her David's at The Blasted Tomato. I'll be there for at least an hour and a half. Tell her she can come on by if she gets the chance. I owe her one."

Nate Newell was sitting with a young black guy with a shiny shaven head, a sad face, and antic smile. They were hogging a sequestered corner table designed for eight. The red vinyl cushion arced like a half moon. Nate sat in the middle, twisting a straw. The other guy rattled ice at the top of the crescent. The table was awash with glasses. The mashed and mixed remnants of a Super Deluxe Nacho Supreme were spewed in the middle. Gashed guacamole, globbed sour cream, shredded yellow cheese, splattered salsa, and sprinkled leeks lay like carnage atop a gouged battlefield of refried beans, greasy ground beef, and smashed tortilla chips. I sat at the bottom of the crescent.

"David, meet Harry Wilson. He's with the theater department for a six-week residency. He's directing *Iceman*."

I pushed up and shook hands across the battlefield. I knew him from somewhere. But it was becoming harder to distinguish between people I'd actually met and those I merely saw on stage, screen, or television.

"Weren't you in *Hurlyburly*?"

"Yeah, I was in the traveling show that came through L.A. last fall. I played Billy."

"That's right. I liked the play. Nice to meet you." I looked at Nate. "Who's our waitress?"

"We got a waiter. A new guy. He must be wearing his invisibility cloak. Next time I see him, I'm ordering two drinks."

"That's him," Harry pointed, his head bobbing. He waved both hands. The waiter came over. Each of us ordered two drinks. I went with their Fetzer Cabernet. All the reports indicated that red wine busted arterial plaque. I spun the plastic cube that held the snack menu. I passed over their heart attack burgers and studied Healthy Favorites.

"I'll take the Right-For-Life salad. Hold the tofu but give me extra carrots and another handful of alfalfa sprouts."

I shoved the cube toward the center of the table. It bulldozed through some vagrant chips but was stopped by a dollop of sour cream.

"What were you doing in the emergency room?" Nate asked. "I hope it's not the heart. Guys our age, we gotta worry about the heart." His forehead wrinkled. His mouth twitched at the corner. Nate was preoccupied by sudden heart attacks. Late last fall, his father had checked into a hospital in Clearwater, Florida, complaining about chest pains. He'd had a mild infarct. The next morning, they'd scheduled a cardiac catheterization, but during the night, on a trip to the bathroom, Ray Newell dropped dead. When the nurse found him, he had been a ghost for at least an hour. Since November, Nate had been taking out his grief by writing a book of poems about fathers. It's called *That Father Lost, Lost His*. Nate had to tell me where he stole the title. It's from *Hamlet*, from where the hypocrite king, who killed Hamlet's father, tells Hamlet he's unmanly and obstinate for being so aggrieved. All fathers die. It's built into the scheme of things—nature's way—and no big deal.

"I don't think it was my heart," I said. My fingers slithered inside my shirt, working over the spaces between the ribs and feeling for the steady beat, beat, beat. I couldn't find it. "More like the brain. I think there's something wrong in my head. I had a near syncope."

Nate groaned.

"What's that?" Harry wondered.

"I almost fainted."

The drinks came.

"What did they do?" Nate was twisting a napkin into knots.

"The basics. Nothing high tech. I didn't even get to see a real doctor. I only got a physician's assistant."

"They're all bastards," Nate seethed. He was bitter. Doctors hadn't saved his father.

"Wait'll you see the bill," Harry barked. "It'll look like a team of surgeons removed buckets of glass from all over your body. Last year, I was peeling an apple and almost sliced my thumb off. The bill was two pages long. All they did—some medical student cleaned it out and stitched it up. He did a lousy job." Harry held up his thumb. "The seam's crooked."

I turned to Nate.

"I didn't have any symptoms. The guy said, 'Wait'll you get some symptoms.'"

"If it was me," Nate said, "I'd check into the Mayo Clinic. You don't want to end up like my old man." His forehead crunched into crooked lines. "He'd been warned, the son of a bitch. For months, he thought he had heartburn. He wouldn't get checked. Just chewed those Tums." Nate gulped his drink. "The book's coming along. I've almost finished the section of twenty-one sonnets." He turned to Harry. "The sonnets are about achieving manhood. I do new variations on the old child-is-the-father-to-the-man motif. Twenty-one fucking times. A sonnet for every year."

One of Nate's problems was he carried unfinished poems around with him. I was sure he had a few on him right now. If he got shook up enough, he'd unfold his hand-edited print-outs, plop them in the guacamole, and start reading.

I looked at Harry. "I tell Nate to count his blessings. His old man went in a flash. He had an easy time becoming a ghost."

Nate snorted. "You and your ghosts! I'd welcome ghosts, but there's one little problem: when you're dead, you're dead. You cease to exist."

Nate gulped some more. His fingers twitched. He was getting ready to yank out some verse. I ignored him—you either believe in ghosts or you don't—sipped my wine and looked at Harry.

"My old man had seventeen days of high-tech death. He was under observation for a heart valve problem that caused an irregular beat. A jolt of cardiac arrest should have done him in, but they got him on a respirator. I got there twelve hours after his collapse. The respirator made his chest jerk. The tube cut the edges of his mouth. They had him drugged and lightly restrained. When the drugs started wearing off, he'd wave his hands, t'ai chi fashion, and loll his head. All the tubes rattled. He'd open his eyes, but I don't think he could see me. He had this hunted look. At one point they had fifteen different drugs going in. I spent seven days holding his hand, reading meters, and watching his urine bag fill. When it stopped filling, his body blew up like a fat suit. They put him on dialysis. He had a machine to breathe, another to clean his blood. There were digital meters for his heart rate, his blood pressure, his blood oxidation level. There was probably a tube in there that could tell you what the stock market was doing. All this went on for seventeen days."

The waiter materialized with my salad. It resembled a pile of hay. I stuffed my mouth.

"That looks good," Harry laughed. "It makes you want to eat." He told the waiter "I'll take a double burger. Rare."

I swallowed.

"The point is," I said, turning to Nate, "he hung on and suffered to no real advantage. Every now and then, he'd shake his head or nod, like he knew my sister and I were there, but he never woke up. I think he was in a state of spiritual disarray. He was neither on one side of the line nor the other. When he passed over, it probably took him a long time to get adjusted." I turned to Harry. "According to my sister, three nights after he died, he appeared to her. He was standing in her walk-in closet. He had his favorite shirt on, the one with the big white and blue horizontal stripes. He didn't say anything. He just tilted his head, looking sad."

"I told you before," Nate blurted, "she had a fucking dream."

"Loni said she was awake. She read the clock and looked at his face and said, 'Don't go, Daddy. Stay with me.' Daddy went. He backed into the closet. When they return like that, it means they're having a hard time adjusting."

"That's spooky," Harry said. "I guess it flipped your sister out."

"As a matter of fact, it was one of the best experiences of her life. She hadn't been able to sleep. Not a wink for three nights—"

"Delirious," Nate laughed. "Hallucinations!"

"—and then she went right out."

I stuffed another pitchfork of dry weeds. A rumpus erupted near the corner of the bar. A fist punched a blond head. The blond guy swung a beer bottle. From across the room, bouncers burrowed through the crowd.

"It must be me," Harry said. "Everywhere I go, fights break out. It's worse than New York."

"They're animals!" Nate growled. "They don't realize how fragile their bodies are."

A brawny black bouncer with dreads had the blond guy by the throat, dragging him toward the door.

"That blond guy is Ashcroft," I said. "He's an actor."

"That figures," Harry laughed. "He looks like a guy I worked with in *The Last Fix*. It was an off-off play. In the middle of the run, he shows up and doesn't know anybody. He's real happy, like a drunk, though we all thought drugs. When he collapses, we're sure it's drugs. He's in this coma for five days and then just wakes up. He's fine. It turns out he had cat scratch fever. The wrong kitty scratches you and you're almost gone."

"That's nothing," Nate said. The waiter zoomed in and plopped down Harry's mooing burger. "You can't even get real constipated anymore. There's this big guy in the History department. Last Friday, in the middle of class, he doubles over and curls up on the floor. Students scream. Tom Fox is groaning, clutching his guts, and some dope tries CPR. Broke his goddamn sternum. The medics cart him off. In the emergency room, they find his big ass puffed up and hard as a rock. They try to drain this infection and realize his bowel had ruptured, so it's into surgery with him. They had to put him on a bag and they still haven't gotten ahead of the infection. A friend of mine visited him yesterday. He said the room had your basic outhouse stench. You could hear Tom's insides gurgle."

I forked through my hay and raked shredded carrots. Harry chomped his burger. Drips of blood drooled on his fries.

"How old's the guy?" I asked.

"Our age. Maybe younger."

I shoveled some chickpeas. You wouldn't think we'd be running down so soon, but we were, some slowly and others in a rush. I told the waiter to bring more hay. It couldn't hurt.

When the waiter was taking the empty plates, Delilah Faye appeared at the side of the table. She was smiling and wearing a fancy turquoise sweat suit. Her butch black hair was pushed up by a turquoise headband. It was a good thing she got there. Our conversation had skittered up and down the critical list. The matter of Tom Fox's colostomy reminded Harry of Jim Bellow's colon cancer and then we tumbled through a freefall of small and large miseries—the people we knew with intussusceptions, kidney stones, acromegaly, lupus, and AIDS.

"Hey!" I said. "It's good to see you. I'm sorry I missed you, but I had to get checked out."

"That's all right, Mr. Sick Man. I just shot over to my club and worked out. I'm famished. Move over and let me sit down."

I wiggled toward Nate and brushed the spilled sprouts into a pile. I made the introductions.

"Since we're away from the set, you can all call me by my real name. I'm Harriet Dombrowski. Delilah Faye's a joke I got stuck with. It started with my father being almost famous in

Milwaukee for doing plumbing supply ads on TV. When I got my first stage part, I picked a ridiculous name. When the parts kept coming, I thought it would be bad luck to change it."

"I'm related to someone almost famous," I said. "Francis Higginson came to the new world in 1630 and wrote an essay back to England about how great the weather was. One day, he went out in the dampness, caught a cold, and died. No lie. The American literature books print his weather report and make him look like a fool. My sister found this out. She's a genealogy nut."

Harriet put her hand to my forehead.

"By the way, why'd you almost faint?"

"How'd you know I had a near syncope?"

"Mary. At my service. She's a big fan of the show. She was impressed when I told her what you did."

"Let's get her over here," Nate grumbled. "Join the party."

"She should be more impressed by you," I said. "You're going to be one of our stars."

"I'll be a star if I don't get hacked out of the show."

"Not a chance," I said. "Eventually, you might *want* to get written out, but as far as we're concerned, you're in line to be a contract regular. Two weeks ago, the producers gave us the word: the show will always need an anorexic, lesbian lawyer. We've got you blocked out on the story board. After the litigation's over and you get Desiree off on a technicality, your anorexia and bulimia will get out of control. You'll almost die. You'll linger in a coma for a few weeks and then you'll open your eyes and want to eat. After you're on your feet again is when you'll have an affair with your therapist. She's going to be a cross-dresser and resemble Roseanne Barr."

Harry piped up. "All this stuff makes O'Neill seem bland."

"With O'Neill," Nate slurred, "you get the essence of the universe and it only takes two hours. What David's describing is pop sludge that'll take months and months to unfold. A lot of people'll be dead by then."

"There's nothing to worry about," I told her. "There'll be plenty of work with the show."

"That's good," she said, "because this is a big break."

"How long you been in La La Land?" Nate wondered.

"About a year. I left Milwaukee last February. Relatively speaking, I'm new at acting. It's what I got into on a whim. I thought I was going to die."

"Don't we all," Nate mumbled.

"No, I had something for real. I didn't just almost faint."

"What happened?" I asked. I liked that she was laughing at me.

"I was a journalism grad from Marquette with a dream job in public relations for the Milwaukee Brewers. One day I started itching all over. I got night sweats. I lost weight. I found a lump under my arm. It turned out to be Hodgkin's disease."

"Damn!" I said. "That's terrible. But you're here."

Bright light flashed from her satin turquoise folds.

"I'm glad to be here. I'm supposedly cured. Hodgkin's is pretty curable. But I had to do six months of chemo and some radiation. My hair fell out. I was sick to my stomach. I promised myself if I got better, I'd do something wild. When my hair grew back, I started going to local casting calls and getting some parts. After I got a big part in a Chicago show, I got my father to stake me. I drove to L.A., found an agent, and did some commercials and extra stuff. I was a murder victim on *CSI: Miami*. I got this part in *Dawn*. Now my agent's getting a lot of calls."

"That's a good story," I said.

"A real Hollywood minute," Nate grumped.

"I've been in remission for five years. I don't worry about it. I'm into life. By the way, I'm famished. What should I have?"

"Everything's okay," I said, "but nothing's very good."

Nate was rumbling some papers. His head was listing. He wanted to give a reading.

"I know you must be disturbed about your health," Harriet

said, turning toward me, "but what's the worst that could happen? You faint and hit the deck. If you wake up, you move on. If you don't, you're in the next world. You find out all the secrets."

Nate groaned and told Harry, "David's got a companion spiritualist." He turned toward Harriet and me. "I don't believe in any of that crap. All I believe in is art. I'm a poet, not a fucking poetaster. This is from *That Father Lost, Lost His.* I'll give you my nineteenth sonnet. It's about when my old man kicked my ass out of the house for smoking pot. I was nineteen at the time. He was right to do it. Here goes."

Five weeks have gone by and I have yet to drop dead or even have another near syncope. A few days after my episode, I went to my personal Medicine Man and took a lot of tests. Blood cultures to the max. The poking of the prostate. Two kinds of cardiograms. Stress tests. Eventually, I even took a CAT scan. There's nothing wrong with me. No one knows why I almost fainted.

Lately, I've been trying to figure out how to round off this story. One of the reasons I'm so fond of Charles Dickens is that after nine hundred pages and seven or eight plots you don't have any more questions. There's nothing left to tell. *Finis.* It's over. In writing my brand of sophisticated hand wringing, I never get to do endings; in soap opera land, new complications spin naturally from old woes. Trouble keeps happening. Like now. I'm on the set, watching a taping, jotting these words and listening as Tiffany Morganchild explains legal strategy to Dawn Desiree.

Tiffany: "I met with Judge Hathorne. Basically, he wants to make an example of you. He said, 'Remember Lorena Bobbitt? Just because she got off doesn't mean it's open season on the male member.'"

[Dawn laughs and picks up a piece of chocolate.]

Dawn: "Does he know we have him on videotape? Going

into the motel room with that seventeen-year-old male prosti-
tute? Tell him the blind wasn't all the way down."

Tiffany: "Don't worry. I was giving him a chance to be a
nice boy about it. Tomorrow, I'll get tough. I've already given
Eddie Ranchero the money. When I put Hathorne on the line,
Eddie will be ready to sing."

The fun is just beginning. Next week, Eddie Ranchero will
mysteriously disappear. It will take another month of shows
for the case to be dismissed. Delilah Faye's performance as
Tiffany Morganchild is a big hit, though there isn't much
to say about Harriet Dombrowski, except we are becoming
friends. We tried kissing once, but it didn't go anywhere. Safe
sex never became an issue. On other fronts, Nate is drinking
more and writing a string of sestinas. I worry about him. Harry Wilson's *Iceman* had a very successful run. Last week, he
went back to New York—to get away from the fights, he said.

I may have to give up and admit my story has no ending.
Things keep happening. For one thing, I've been having a lot
of odd dreams. A few nights ago, a forest gathered into the
sky and then four houses slid down a canyon. On the beach, I
watched and listened while strangers played chess and argued
in a foreign language. Early this morning, I woke up from one
of the strangest. I was jogging midmorning on the quake-rav-
aged Santa Monica Freeway. At my side was a shrunken man
in a motorized wheelchair. He had the face of my father.
Wrapped in a baggy gray sweat suit, he was laughing hard. His
head seemed as large as a watermelon. It tilted toward me, his
mouth churning, chuckling, and guffawing. Through all the
laughter, he was speaking. I can't remember the words, but he
was talking and laughing, and I was listening, all serious, trying
to hear what he was saying, running to keep up, and watching
the highway for large holes. I was worried we were going to
fall through.

I woke up then and couldn't get back to sleep. It was 5:33. I
lay there, waiting for the day, wondering why the clock blinked

so slowly, why nothing moved. I found myself not sleeping or dreaming but drifting, wondering about the laughing man with my father's face, and imagining a whole freeway full of laughing cripples, a parade of the physically challenged, complete with floats and wheeling musicians. There would be a section for rolling hospital beds and racing gurneys, a street ballet with no end in sight. The parade would go on and on, a stream of human joy. There would be no tripping, fainting, or dying. No flesh failures. Everyone would be out for the day. There would be no one hanging by a thread, not a single name on the critical list.

John Stenwick yells, "Cut."

The lighting's not right. Two technicians scramble to adjust the standing floods. We'll need another take. No one minds. This is business. It occurs to me to slip out and call Nate Newell and tell him about my latest dream. I will have to assure him that I did not see my father as a ghost, that it was only a dream. It will be my job to get Nate laughing. He needs to do more laughing, but I will wait until after the last take, wait for Dawn and Tiffany to finish conspiring beneath corrected lighting. The actors are moving into place. For a little while, I'll sit still, shut my eyes, and watch the beds roll, the gurneys dance, and the wheelchairs glide. Along the shattered expressway, the infirm will laugh, and the silent music will play. It's all about to happen. Now, *finis*.

ACKNOWLEDGENTS

The stories in this collection first appeared in the following publications:

"Choke Hold" *Delmarva Quarterly*
"Closets" *North Atlantic Review*
"House Arrest" *Cimarron Review*
"Mulekick" *The Chariton Review*
"Z-Man and the Christmas Tree" *The Chariton Review*
"A Good Samaritan Will Stop" *The Montreal Review*
"The Jolly Season" *Chesapeake East*
"The Decomposing Log" *Words of Wisdom*
"Young Mr. Moyen" *Blue Lake Review*
"Baby" *Timber Creek Review*
"Anchorite" *RiverSedge*
"The Critical List" *Writers' Forum*